The Mission of Mooney Rooney

by
David and Samuel Luke

Bloomington, IN Milton Keynes, UK
authorHOUSE®

AuthorHouse™
1663 Liberty Drive, Suite 200
Bloomington, IN 47403
www.authorhouse.com
Phone: 1-800-839-8640

AuthorHouse™ UK Ltd.
500 Avebury Boulevard
Central Milton Keynes, MK9 2BE
www.authorhouse.co.uk
Phone: 08001974150

This book is a work of fiction. People, places, events, and situations are the product of the author's imagination. Any resemblance to actual persons, living or dead, or historical events, is purely coincidental.

© 2007 David and Samuel Luke. All rights reserved.

No part of this book may be reproduced, stored in a retrieval system, or transmitted by any means without the written permission of the author.

First published by AuthorHouse 6/7/2007

ISBN: 978-1-4259-9522-5 (sc)

Printed in the United States of America
Bloomington, Indiana

This book is printed on acid-free paper.

Contents

1. The Black Sphere 1
2. Mooney 4
3. The Red Butterfly 9
4. The Amazing Boy from England 14
5. The Halo of Friendship 24
6. The Long Journey 33
7. The Mission of Mooney 41
8. The Guide 46
9. Aetheria 53
10. The Training 64
11. The Translucent Chamber 77
12. The Plan 87
13. The Ündian Hiding 96
14. The Encounter 105
15. The Highest of Aetheria 111
16. Farewell 116
17. Greetings, Mr. Presidents 122
18. Home 130
19. Ündia 140
20. The City under Water 149
21. The Secret of the Laboratory 160
22. The Spirit Spheres 171
23. The Map 178
24. Cave Behind Waterfall 187
25. The Hengestone 197

Chapter 1
The Black Sphere

It was another unquiet night in March 2003, when neon signs melted the city of Las Vegas, and gamblers threw themselves heedlessly into the frenzy of chances. Idle, yet ungentle, something paid a visit to the countryside of the city. This thing was, strange indeed, a tornado.

It was hanging ten feet above the bare plain beyond the woods. Instead of a funnel, it was shaped like a ten-yard wide round pillar reaching down from the sky. Although the air inside the tornado was visibly twirling upwards at a great speed, the earth around its base didn't seem to have moved at all. Together with silver sparkles, there was red light, mysterious yet beautiful, that pierced through the wall of the tornado, making the whole thing so bright that it could be seen even from Las Vegas city.

Driven by curiosity, people who saw the light hopped into their cars and drove to the countryside. As they got nearer to the tornado, they felt a strong heat wave coming towards them through their windshields, forcing them to stop their vehicles some fifty yards away from the wind pillar. The visitors had absolutely no idea of what was in front of them, and were lost for words.

Very soon after that night, the wind pillar caught the attention of the local government. Police cars swarmed the area, forcing spectators to leave due to security reasons. A top national scientist also arrived with his group. His name was Ince, a half bald climatologist who looked slightly obese and clumsy in his grey-blue jacket and a twisted necktie. Excited about his new research, Dr. Ince adjusted his thin, black rimmed spectacles constantly and surveyed the place with special equipments. The scientists had quickly set up a temporary research station near the wind pillar; but after 24 hours of hard work, they were still scratching their heads before the strange thing – they had not come across anything like this before in their entire lives.

Suddenly, when the researchers were about to get some sleep in their tents, a transformation occurred to the tornado: it turned from a pillar of wind into a vertical beam of light. Since the heat around it had ceased a little, Dr. Ince, together with the other scientists and policemen, tried to walk near it, but felt a strong force and even greater heat than before as they reached about two yards in front of it. The force pushed them back and nearly knocked them over. Looking up into the beam of light, Dr. Ince now saw a huge sphere about fifteen feet in diameter, floating still among the pale red light in the center of the beam. This sphere was black on the outside; although it looked solid, Dr. Ince declared that it didn't resemble any kind of metal, stone or wood. Nobody knew what it was.

Dr. Ince feared the potential danger of the Black Sphere and ordered his men to take a closer look at it using a tower ladder. But other than the fact that the Sphere had a 'flawless' surface, the men could report nothing more.

'What should I do? What should I do?' panicked Dr. Ince. For another 24 hours, he tried to enter the Pillar using varies methods, but he went back to the station without any reward. He wanted to cry,

2

The Mission of Mooney Rooney

realizing that he was representing the country that claimed itself to be the world's best in science and technology.

This strange object had been popular on the news, of course, being suspected as an "U.F.O. of some sort." However, the Pillar of Light anchored at the same spot months after its appearance and never took any further changes. The public had gradually lost interest in it.

Now the countryside of Las Vegas had been made inhibitory by the government, while Dr. Ince was commanded to stay at the research station with his team until critical discoveries were made.

Chapter 2
Mooney

On the west side of Vancouver, BC, Canada, there laid a quiet, tiny community called Kerrisdale. It was a peaceful neighbourhood, an ideal dwelling place for seniors as well as small young families. Mooney Rooney, thirteen, lived there with his parents, and went to Point Grey Secondary School ten blocks away from his house.

It was a cool Friday morning in May, when Mooney left home for school. Sweet breeze welcomed his fair face and gave life to his hair of crimson. He wasn't tall for his age, but there was an unspeakable magic about his eyes that seem to make him shine attractively with vitality. He was a good talker, too, and all the older grades loved him. But there was one thing about this grade eight boy that all hated and feared: his nasty tricks on his fellow classmates. Today, he had brought with him a small wooden box to his first class.

Mooney found himself early in his usual seat beside his classmate Mitsie. 'Hey Mitsie,' said Mooney in a faithful and charming voice. 'Your hair looks totally lovely this morning. I ah…brought a little gift with me. It's for the cutest girl I see today. Well Mitsie, I think you very much deserve this gift!'

The Mission of Mooney Rooney

'Oh Mooney...' The girl received the wooden box from Mooney and blushed. 'Open it,' said Mooney.

Mitsie carefully untied the yellow ribbon and opened the box. All she could remember was Mooney's burst of laughter, and the image of three black cockroaches crawling out of the box, waving their hairy antennae at her. Her face turned pale, and tears went straight down her cheeks.

Mooney whispered something in the corner of his lips, and immediately the three cockroaches flew toward the face of poor Mitsie. Mitsie sprang back with horror and fell to the ground, knocking down the tables behind her and jerking the whole class into madness. Now Mooney whispered again, and the cockroaches flew out of the window and were gone. Mooney Rooney had made a mess out of his class, again, and he wouldn't stop laughing.

In the office of the school's vice-principal, Mooney stood fearless in front of the furious Mr. Martin: he was just too used to situations like this.

'Mooney!' said Mr. Martin. 'I'm tired of asking you the same question over and over again: how do you control those insects? Earwigs, carpenter ants, flies...now cockroaches! If you tell me the truth now, you're free from garbage duty.'

'It's "grounds cleanup," Mr. Martin,' said Mooney, 'and I feel very honoured to do it for the school.'

*   *   *

Mooney was especially talented in music, and had been playing the piano since grade four. One evening last year, Mooney was playing a classical piece on his piano at home, absorbing himself totally into his own world. With eyes closed, he wasn't being conscious of what was going on around him: dragonflies, bees, butterflies, beetles...hundreds

5

of beautiful creatures flew slowly into his house from the windows, landing one by one on Mooney's piano.

Awaking from his reverie, Mooney saw a rare dragonfly with red and green stripes resting on his shoulder. 'I've got you here eh?' said Mooney, who had read books about insects out of interest. But as he looked straight in front of him, he was shocked to see the entire surface of his piano being covered by winged insects of vibrant colors, and that all of their eyeballs were fixed on him. He fell to the ground, wordless; and behold! the floor of his house had turned into a sea of crawling insects that stared at him with their bead-like eyes...

*　*　*

Mooney's mom had been working at a lawyer's firm since Mooney was grade six, and she valued her job on top of everything. Although she came home every evening to prepare for dinner, she spent little time with her only child Mooney, thinking that he was already old enough to take care of himself, and that a woman should focus on her career if she had any.

Mooney's dad was the owner of a realty company, and, like his wife, he was very much devoted to his work. After his graduation from university, he got married under the pressure of his own parents and started a career in a small realty company, slowly beginning to build his own business. He wasn't a romantic person, as Mooney had perceived, and didn't have a clear concept of what a family should be.

The relationship between Mooney and his parents wasn't close. They said 'hi' when they saw each other, though, but seldom talked. One of the few times they talked was about buying a piano. Mooney's dad objected it at first; but under his own realization of the child's genius, the family bought home a second-hand piano. From then on, since Mooney was home alone almost every day, he had not only discovered

The Mission of Mooney Rooney

his own musical world, but had also developed the ability to think and solve problems independently. But on the other side of the coin, he had also grown into a self-centered character.

* * *

...With his mouth wide open, Mooney was sitting on the floor among the insects. As if an enchantment had befallen the hour, Mooney started to hear a melody whispering in the air. It was an unknown, unique style of music, which Mooney had never heard before. As he began to sing along the melody, he seemed to understand what the insects were thinking about – after a while, he could even communicate with the creatures, singing the same notes from the melody though of different patterns. He felt as if he and the insects were acquainted long ago, even before he could remember. Mooney could never forget this experience, and he kept it to himself.

* * *

Mooney remembered the first time when he brought earwigs to school and ended up in Mr. Martin's office.

'So...your classmates say that you ordered the bugs to attack them,' said Mr. Martin. 'Is that true?'

'Do you believe in such nonsense?' said Mooney. 'I don't know, Mr. Martin. Those earwigs were my pets, and they just came out of my bag when those bullies pushed me down onto the floor. I didn't order them to come out, you see. And you should charge those guys for bullying!'

What Mooney said was actually half right. There were many bullies at school, and the administration just kept ignoring them. Sometimes Mooney's tricks were justified even by other students, who admired him in secret. He also had good grades, and that was why the school didn't want to expel him despite the boy's misconducts, for the sake of its own academic reputation. After all, Mooney had no real friends; he was always alone, and he liked it better that way.

One morning before school, Mooney was having breakfast with his parents.

'Mom told me that there was a phone call from school, saying that you played tricks on other kids. Is that right?' asked Mr. Rooney.

Mooney wiped the milk off his chin with his sleeve.

'They said you can control bugs...well I don't really believe that, neither does your mom.'

'Honey,' said his mother, 'I know you can take care of yourself very well, and I trust you. But at least, give me an explanation so that I can talk to the school...'

'You know what?' said Mooney. 'People have their own tongues and are granted the freedom of speech. Let them say whatever they want to say. I was just playing with my friends – that was all. And you know I keep bugs as pets, and sometimes they just escape. It's fine, mom, I can talk it over with the school.'

'I'm just worried that you're making enemies at school, hon,' said Mrs. Rooney, already packing for work.

'Enemies? Mom, don't you worry about me,' said Mooney. 'I love school.' He gulped.

'That's good then,' said Mrs. Rooney with a quick smile.

After breakfast, Mooney and his dad left the house together. 'Well Mooney, you should teach me how to control bugs someday – I'd like to use it against those irritating clients!' This started their day with laughter. After that morning, Mooney's parents were busy with their work again and paid no more attention to the phone calls from school. Peacefully, Mooney's life dragged on with his music and his little insect friends.

Chapter 3
The Red Butterfly

Summer had come – there were only a few days left for school. The weather was getting adorable for baseball, and all the people in Kerrisdale were delighted to embrace the sweetness of summer.

Mooney was alone walking home from school. As usual, instead of the busy 41st Avenue where people shopped along, Mooney took the 39th Avenue, preferring its quietness. His heart was light for the coming of summer, and he whistled along his way.

As he looked up to a maple tree on the sidewalk, he saw something twinkling among the leaves under the sunshine. So he walked closer, and found that it was a butterfly as big as his palm, having wings that were bright red in colour. Gazing at the strange creature sitting up high on the branch, Mooney had a sudden illusion that it was going to dive into his face and consume everything inside him. He tried to communicate with the insect, but to his surprise, he couldn't exchange any thoughts with it at all.

Now the butterfly had moved to another tree nearby and stopped there, seemingly to be waiting for Mooney to come after it. As Mooney came closer to it again, it flew to yet another tree – after a while, it became obvious to Mooney that the butterfly was leading him to somewhere. With curiosity tickling, he followed tightly after it, and paid no attention to where he was going.

Finally, he saw the red wings coming to a stop on the second-floor balcony of a small white house. There were delicate flowers planted in pots on the balcony; the house itself looked plain with a light blue roof and a perfect front lawn.

'Haha…look who's here!'

Mooney turned around and saw Mitsie's older brother, Bert, with two other boys from school. 'What are you doing here, you little worm?' said Bert.

'I do whatever I like, and it's none of your business,' said Mooney. He looked back to the balcony and saw that the red butterfly was gone.

'None of my business?' said Bert. 'What about my sister then? She's none of your business.' Mooney ignored him and ran across the street, but both of Bert's friends were there before him. 'What's up, worm? We want to see your skills.' And now Mitsie had come out of the small white house following Bert's terrible yell.

Mooney was busy looking around for insects, but all he could find was a few small flies. He quickly muttered some unknown music, telling the flies to aim for the boys' faces and distract them – but one of Bert's friends revealed the bottle of pesticide that he was hiding behind his back and sprayed it at the poor flies, which fell to the ground and died in two seconds.

'That's all you've got, eh?' said Bert, rolling up his sleeves as he walked slowly towards Mooney. 'Well, I'll let you see what I've got right here!'

'There!' cried a voice, like bell, out of nowhere. 'Don't you bully on such a helpless kid!'

The Mission of Mooney Rooney

Mooney then turned and saw a girl – a gorgeous blonde girl with a ponytail, standing erect on the edge of the balcony where the red butterfly was resting some minutes ago. She was wearing a white t-shirt and a pair of tight red jeans that highlighted her muscular yet attractive body curves. Smiling in her slightly freckled face, she jumped off the balcony like a cat, landing on the lawn with an amazingly light weight and perfect balance.

'Sherlyn, please, leave us alone...' said Bert with a weak voice.

'Very well – but Bert, this kid is standing on my lawn, and he might, very possibly, be my dad's guest. You know what's going to happen if you mess with me and my dad, don't you?' As she talked, it seemed to Mooney that her cheeks glowed like lilies in the sun.

Sherlyn's father was a rude, hulking drunk, and everybody in the neighbourhood feared and avoided him. Upon hearing Sherlyn speaking of her father, Bert and his friends already stepped back a bit. 'Daddy–!' Sherlyn yelled.

'You're lucky this time, Mooney Wormy – but not next time!' As the gang started to hurry back to Mitsie's house across the street, they heard something hissing behind their back – a huge swarm of wasps were heading straight towards them. Scared to death, Bert and his friends sprinted with their greatest strength and headed home for their lives, being lucky to have made it just in time.

Sherlyn bent her slender body and laughed. But she looked up at the departing wasps and paused: the coming of the insects couldn't be an accident, she thought. She turned her head and looked at Mooney, face to face for the first time – and when their eyes met they both felt a stream of chill, then warmth, rushing slowly up their cheeks from their guts and down to their toes. Mooney smiled and turned away for home.

'Hey, wait! You haven't even thanked me for saving your life,' Sherlyn caught up with Mooney and walked side by side with him.

'You called me a "kid," ' said Mooney. 'A "helpless kid." '

'I'm sorry.'

'Your name's…Sherlyn?'

'Yeah. I go to Magee, grade eight. And your name? "Wormy"?'

'Mooney,' he smiled. 'I go to Point Grey. I'm in grade eight, too. So were you scared when the wasps came?'

'Of course not,' said Sherlyn. 'They weren't even aiming for me. Why? Did you…?'

Mooney looked at Sherlyn again, and realized a feeling he had never had before. He had long been living alone in his own world, and had longed for a friend and companion who would know him well and trust him. Now Sherlyn was taking the first step to their friendship, and he was glad. 'Do what? You mean the thing with the wasps?' He said. 'Well, I didn't tell them to attack the bullies – just to scare them away.' When Sherlyn was talking to Bert, Mooney found several wasps flying among the flowers on Mitsie's balcony, and so he asked them to bring along their friends for Bert.

Sherlyn was a little frightened to hear about that at first, but she didn't fear Mooney after all, since she was special herself, too. 'Well then,' she said. 'I think you didn't really need my help.'

'Uh…I couldn't have done it without you,' said Mooney. 'You saved me from being beaten up.'

Sherlyn was still not satisfied with his answer – all she wanted was a 'thank you'. 'Okay then, Mooney,' she said. 'I've got to go home now, see you!'

But all of a sudden Mooney seemed to have pulled himself out of the conversation. He was thinking about that strange butterfly: why couldn't I communicate with it, he thought. Why did it lead me to trouble and then disappeared? And, was there something between the red wings of the butterfly and the red jeans of Sherlyn?

12

The Mission of Mooney Rooney

'Oh...bye,' said Mooney with an awkward smile. Finally, the girl couldn't resist herself and asked, 'It's Saturday tomorrow. I'm free for the whole day. Should I come to your house and hear about your special power?'

Mooney nearly jumped up with joy. After exchanging phone numbers with Sherlyn, he ambled home, looking forward to the end of the day.

Chapter 4
The Amazing Boy from England

It had been two weeks since Mooney and Sherlyn came to know each other. They met almost every day after summer break had started, and they talked a lot. Sherlyn's full name was Sherlyn Claxton, and she was a lonely child, too. She was born in the States, and her biological father died a long time ago. After her mother got married to her stepfather, a Canadian, the whole family moved to Vancouver when Sherlyn was still in kindergarten. After her half brother was born, her mother paid all her attention to the baby and his father and didn't care much about Sherlyn. Since little, Sherlyn seemed to have an invincible amount of energy and excelled in every sport she played. She could run faster than anyone could imagine and jump like a frog to an amazing height and distance. Scared of suspicion, she had to hide her special abilities while playing sports. Although she had always been popular at school because of her outstanding talents and appearance, she didn't have any real friends due her extraordinary ("weird" as her classmates called it) way of thinking. Now that she had met Mooney, another lonely, special person – perfect! She felt that she could talk about anything with him.

It was Thursday today, and Sherlyn was at Mooney's house listening to him playing the piano. On Sherlyn's suggestion of having some insects as their company, Mooney keyed out some strange melodies on the piano, filled the house slowly with butterflies. And as he started to play a romantic waltz, the butterflies raised and lowered themselves in the air along with the rhythm, as if becoming one with the music. Sherlyn, inspired by such scenery, began to dance, too. She had never danced before, but because of her special talent, she leapt and fell among the butterflies and produced incredible dexterity. Abruptly, Mooney pulled his fingers away from the keyboard, sitting still in front of the unusual dancers. Sherlyn let out a smile and said, 'Hey, why do you stop?'

'That was beautiful,' said Mooney in a dreamy voice. 'I mean…your dancing is too beautiful to watch.' Sherlyn's ears went red.

At this very moment, Mooney saw something like a small fireball entering the house from a window and then quickly leaving from another. 'The red butterfly!' Mooney shouted.

'What red butterfly?' asked Sherlyn.

'Oh – forgot to tell you about it,' said Mooney. 'But follow me! I'll explain it to you along the way.'

The butterfly was heading straight towards West Boulevard. Since it was flying rather slowly, Mooney managed to tell Sherlyn everything about the strange creature as they paced after it. She agreed with his assumption that the butterfly was having a purpose of its own.

The insect turned north at West Boulevard and stopped on a window of the number 16 bus that was waiting at the bus stop: Mooney and Sherlyn crossed the street and hopped onto the bus. Seeing that the butterfly was clinching to the outside of the window at the left back corner of the bus, the two of them seated themselves accordingly. They paid close attention to the insect as the bus started; although the red wings were struck violently by the wind blowing southwards, the insect anchored itself on the glass with its legs and had no signs of falling. When the bus reached Granville Street, the butterfly suddenly detached itself from the glass and flew straight to Granville Bridge. Mooney and Sherlyn got off immediately at the next stop and ran after it.

Granville Bridge was built not only for traffic, but also for people to jog along its sidewalk, viewing over the beautiful creek running between Vancouver and its downtown. The red butterfly rushed to the north; like a flash, it vanished on the middle section of the bridge. Mooney and Sherlyn stopped some yards away from where it disappeared, and saw a thin faced, pale-haired boy standing there, leaning on the fence along the edge of the bridge. Looking about nine years old, the boy weighed his small head heavily on his palms, faintly overlooking the creek with his narrow eyes.

Coming from the south, a truck was speeding along the bridge. It was honking as it swung from side to side, bringing other drivers into panic and the traffic into chaos. As it was about to crash into a car in front of it, its driver turned the steering wheel attempting to change its direction. But the vehicle seemed to have lost control – it hit a car on its bumper, crashed towards the pavement and ran directly at Mooney and Sherlyn. Without thinking, Sherlyn took Mooney by her one arm and pushed on the fence with her other using all her strength, launching Mooney and herself ten yards away from the bridge.

'It's better to fall into the water than get hit by a truck!' Sherlyn held Mooney tight in her arms and dove together through the air.

Just as they were about to hit the water, they felt that they had landed on something soft and smooth. With eyes half open, Mooney reached down his hand and felt silk – it was silk, indeed. Mooney and Sherlyn lifted their heads, and saw the small boy on the bridge now sitting beside them on top of the silky object, and were staring at them

16

with his cheerless eyes. 'Why are you hugging?' He muttered with a British accent. Mooney and Sherlyn sprang away from each other.

Now Mooney found that he was sitting on a thing that would only appear in his ridiculous dreams – a flying cloth! It was red in colour, like burning fire; there were neat, white markings of some unknown language along its woolly margins. Although it was only about nine feet long, two yards wide, and gave way to any weight on its surface, it was stretchable enough to carry three passengers, and possibly more.

The silk cloth looked like a meteor dashing across the sky as it "flies," leaving a blazing red trail behind it which faded away in a half a second. Mooney now found that they had already come to a stop on the hillside in North Vancouver, and that they were resting on the ground under many tall firs.

'What is this...thing?' Mooney asked, pointing at the red cloth. 'Is it yours?'

The boy sat still. Mooney saw that his face was fair, but that it was sorrowful. 'Hey little fellow,' said Mooney, 'you saved my life...I don't know how to repay you. But could you please tell me what happened?' The boy still wouldn't answer.

Our meeting couldn't have been by chance, thought Sherlyn, and we'd for sure be friends in the days to come. 'My name is Sherlyn,' she said, leaning over to the boy, 'and this is my friend Mooney. We want to thank you: if it wasn't you, we could have drowned. And eh, you know, I think this cloth of yours is really amazing – would you like to take us around on it one more time?'

'Okay,' said the boy softly with a bit of pride. 'But not to a place where we can be seen by others.'

'I agree,' Sherlyn said. 'We can fly around this hill then.'

At once the red cloth lifted them into the air. 'Hey, gentle!' laughed Mooney. 'Too fast there little guy. I want to feel like flying. Like a bird.'

Like a bird, the cloth lingered around the hill on top of the tall fir trees. Looking southward, Mooney and Sherlyn saw the beautiful city of Vancouver lying silently across Fraser River beneath the dusk. 'I feel so lucky,' said Sherlyn, 'that I have met two people with special powers in just two weeks.'

'What?' exclaimed the little boy. 'He can fly too?'

'Well, no,' said Sherlyn, 'but he can control insects. Um…by the way, what's your name?'

'Colin. Colin Brandon.'

'Nice to meet you, Colin,' said Sherlyn. 'Mooney, show some of your tricks to Colin, would you? Are you scared of insects, Colin?'

'I'm afraid of spiders.'

'Don't worry,' said Mooney. 'Spiders are not insects.'

So Mooney summoned some moths from the woods below and told them to dance in front of Colin. Some beetles also landed onto the palms of the small boy, who smiled and giggled at the tickling. His grave face had given way to a joyful and innocent one – a face that a child should have.

'I'm kind of hungry,' said Sherlyn. 'Let's go home – we wouldn't want to use the cloth though, it's too obvious. Let's land here and we'll walk down hill.' After they landed, Colin folded the piece of silk carefully and put it back into his backpack.

'Where do you live, Colin?' asked Sherlyn as they walked. Colin lowered his head.

'It's getting late,' she continued. 'Your parents must be worried about you – what were you doing on the bridge by the way?'

As if Sherlyn had said something wrong, Colin stopped walking abruptly. 'I don't want to go home,' he said. 'Can I come to your house and stay?'

The Mission of Mooney Rooney

This request surprised both Mooney and Sherlyn. 'I really don't want to go home!' Colin continued, with tears. 'They're bad people!'

'Oh – so you ran away from home...' said Mooney, who really didn't know how to settle down this little boy.

'It doesn't matter, Colin,' said Sherlyn. 'My parents don't treat me no good either, but I always take it easy.'

'They're not my parents,' said Colin. 'My parents died already. They are my uncle and aunt. I just don't want to go back anymore.'

Mooney thought for a moment and said, 'You can come to my house and stay – it's not a problem in fact. It's summer right now and my parents wouldn't notice.'

'Sounds like a good idea,' said Sherlyn. 'And I live close by – I'll come visit you anytime.'

The boy seemed happy again. He held Sherlyn by his hand, and the three of them walked on.

*   *   *

Mooney brought Colin to his room before his parents came home from work. 'You can hide inside my closet for now – it's big enough for you little kid,' he said. 'You could slide the door open and let some air in. Only come out when my parents are away – are you okay with that?'

'I can handle it,' said Colin.

After dinner, Mooney sneaked up some food for Colin. The two of them found it fun keeping things secret. At night, Colin took out the red cloth from his backpack and unfolded it. He flung it flat, levelling it a foot above the floor and climbed onto it with a blanket from Mooney. With the help from his cloth, Colin found himself just an inch below the ceiling of the room, where he fell soundly asleep in almost no time.

19

The next morning, Sherlyn came to Mooney's house when a few beetles were trying to flip some impossible summersaults for Colin. Carrying a mindful of questions unanswered, Sherlyn sat beside the giggling boy. 'Colin, please don't mind me asking,' she said. 'What happened among you and your uncle and aunt? I'm sure they care about you.'

'Well, I don't know...I mean, they are the only relatives I have left,' said Colin. 'I was born in England and used to live there with my parents. But after my parents died, my uncle and aunt in Canada inherited a lot of our money and fostered me – all because of the money. They don't even like me – at least I don't feel it. But now, I have got you two kind people as my friends...I feel happy again.' His eyes turned red, but Sherlyn smiled and held his hand. Ever since Colin came to Canada, he had been living in the memory of his parents, whom he loved the most. Because of that, he never heeded school or anything that happened to his uncle and aunt (this was, perhaps, one of the factors that led to his strained relationship with them). Now that he had met Mooney and Sherlyn, to whom he could tell everything that was stuffed inside his heart, he felt as if they were his brother and sister, despite the fact that he never had any.

'What are you going to do if your uncle and aunt look for you?' asked Mooney.

'I don't care,' muttered Colin. 'I don't want to see them and they don't want to see me.'

'Aw,' said Sherlyn. 'Well, let's talk about something else – something interesting. Um...how about your...your magic cloth?'

'Sure,' said Colin. 'Actually, I haven't told the story to anyone yet, but I know I should have. I should have let my parents know when they were alive, and I could have travelled in the air with them.' Colin gazed into the sky and sighed. 'When I was about four years old, my parents

20

brought me to some Middle East country for vacation. We were walking along a busy street, where people sold different kinds of exotic fabrics and mats on the floor and in stores along the sidewalk. Suddenly I felt a strong desire to go into one of the stores: I swung off my dad's hand and headed to the store without thinking. I remember seeing a radiance coming from the store, but my parents didn't seem to notice it. But I didn't care. I entered the store instinctively and dug out a red piece of silk from a pile of cheap fabrics. I wouldn't let go of it – I couldn't. Then dad came over and asked if I liked that cloth – I said yes, of course, and he bought it for me. My mom said it was strange for a boy to like that colour, but I didn't care – I just felt that it was mine, that it was part of me. I held it tight in my chest – it was the happiest moment in my life. Since then, I haven't been parted with my cloth.

'When I got home with it, I spread it on my bed and slept on it. After a while, I saw some light appeared on the ceiling above me, and I got up. I looked around and found that the light was in fact coming from the cloth – the cloth was glowing! And since I'd got up, all the light shooting out from the cloth was directed up to the ceiling. I looked into the vertical bundles of light between the cloth and the ceiling and saw some strange, unknown characters floating within. I didn't know what they were at first, but after awhile – I didn't know why – I started reading out the words as if I knew the language since I was born. Those were some spells I guess, some kind of magic spells, because as I read them, the cloth started to move. After some practise, I could totally manipulate the movements of the cloth and use it however I liked.'

'Wow, that's amazing!' said Mooney.

'Does it have a name?' asked Sherlyn.

'A name?' said Colin. 'No.'

'Let's give it a name then,' said Sherlyn. 'Um…it's fast, and it's red…how about: "Blazing Lightning Reddish Swift-Flying Sky-Slashing Amazing Cuddling"…'

21

'Seesh, Sherlyn,' said Mooney, 'what a name. What about "Reddash"?'

'It's weird,' said Sherlyn.

'It doesn't matter,' said Colin, smiling. 'As long as my cloth is with me, I'm happy with whatever you want to call it.'

All of a sudden, Mooney lowered his head and fell into deep thought again. Sherlyn tried to wake him several times, but he didn't seem to notice at all. Finally he caught himself back, and he said, 'The meeting of us three couldn't be by chance. Don't you think that the red butterfly has linked us all together? We always say that there are many people who have special powers in this world, but it is rare for them to get to know each other, even in small numbers. And I have a good feeling about our meeting too – how about you guys?'

'Well, yeah, I think so too,' said Sherlyn. 'To be honest, Mooney, I have been feeling especially comfortable being with you. After I met Colin, that feeling seems to have grown stronger...and it feels like...like...you were myself.' Mooney caught Sherlyn's eyes and quickly looked away.

'How about you, Colin?' asked Sherlyn.

'I don't even know what you are talking about,' said Colin.

'Do you think the butterfly will appear again?' asked Sherlyn, turning to Mooney.

'I don't know,' said Mooney. 'But what I am concerned about the most is the purpose of it bringing us together...'

But they stopped talking about it, realizing that this matter was beyond their measure.

'Colin,' said Sherlyn, 'what if your uncle looks for you? You have gone for more than a day now, and he could have called the police.'

'I don't care,' said Colin.

The Mission of Mooney Rooney

'Well then, let's see if there're any posts about lost kids,' said Mooney, taking out the morning paper. 'Oh look!' he cried. 'The red butterfly's on the news!' Sherlyn rolled over to Mooney at once, but all she saw was an advertisement with a red butterfly sitting on top of a bottle of perfume. Mooney laughed, as Sherlyn tried to tickle him; and for a short while in their minds, it seemed that time had ceased, and that the room was filled with happiness, and the world with peace.

Chapter 5
The Halo of Friendship

It was Saturday morning, and Mooney was having breakfast with his parents. He wrapped up a muffin in a paper towel and was about to bring it up for Colin. 'Mooney!' cried his dad behind the morning newspaper.

'Yes, Dad?' said Mooney, almost dropping the muffin to the floor.

'What's wrong? You seem to be in a hurry all time in the past couple of days,' said Mr. Rooney.

'Oh yeah,' said Mooney. 'I'm just ah…doing some scientific research on – '

'Anyway, it is Charles' birthday today,' said Mr. Rooney with a mouthful of pancake. 'He's holding a little party at his house, and we are invited.'

'Which Charles?'

'Do you remember that Chinese couple named Cheung, who came to our house last time?' said Mrs. Rooney. 'Charles is their son. The family just moved here from China, and dad helped them got a house in Richmond. Now they are just hoping to make some new friends, you know, they're new to Vancouver after all. People from China are really

24

wealthy nowadays. They buy huge houses once they get here. Perhaps Mr. Cheung is going to buy some more houses from dad, eh?'

'Yeah,' said Mr. Rooney. 'And you know, if I can make my name big enough in the Chinese community, then it's my turn to become a billionaire!'

'I don't care about all these,' said Mooney. 'I just don't want to go to that party. I don't even know Charles.'

'For all our sakes, you have to go,' insisted Mr. Rooney.

'Now you're becoming a Chinese parent here, Mr. Billionaire,' said Mooney.

'That's not the best thing to say to your father, Mooney,' said Mrs. Rooney. 'You should go – Charles needs company.'

'Company?' said Mooney. 'Then can bring my friends too if I go?'

'That's alright,' said Mr. Rooney. 'As long as they're good kids.'

'As long as they are good kids? They're my friends, and – '

'Alright,' said Mr. Rooney. 'Tell them to meet here at two o'clock. Don't be late.'

Sherlyn came to Mooney's house at a quarter to two, when Mooney and Colin rushed downstairs to meet her. Mr. Rooney was a little surprised to see Colin coming from upstairs, but Mooney uttered some awkward reasons to him, and everything seemed fine. Mooney and his friends then seated themselves at the back of Mr. Rooney's car and headed for Richmond.

The five of them arrived at Mr. Cheung's house in about twenty minutes. 'This is a really big house!' exclaimed Mooney, tilting his chin up. 'Dad, why do they build such high fences around their lawn? Do they have allergies or something?'

'Mooney!' said his dad frowning. 'The fences are built for security reasons.'

The outer design of the house was somewhat different from those in Vancouver West. With walls painted light pink, the house looked like a huge cement cube with large windows mounted on its sides, like dots on a dice. It must be very spacious inside, thought Mooney.

Mr. Cheung came out of the front door and welcomed them into the house. About twenty guests were already chatting and laughing in the living room, now in English, now in Chinese. Mooney and his friends seated themselves on a couch at the corner of the room, feeling extremely uneasy.

A boy with a chunk of spiky blonde hair came over to them. 'Hi, I'm Charles,' said the boy, swaying his head a bit as he tried to show off his metal hoop earrings. He was twelve, and he was wearing a pair of jeans with holes and thorns. 'I'm your host today. Me and my father love to make friends, and you please feel at home. Just give me a shout if you need any help.'

'We don't need no help,' said Sherlyn, giving him a glare. 'But we want to go somewhere quiet – our ears hurt.'

'Help yourselves,' said Charles, twitching his lips. 'My house is big – not hard to find a quiet place.'

Before Sherlyn could say anything, Mr. Cheung came to them with a warm smile. 'Mooney!' he said. 'I heard your father said you play good piano. Come, I show you my piano – I bought it only for decoration. We don't play. Now you play, will you? I don't want to leave it here untouched.' Mooney was about to say no, but Sherlyn winked and said, 'Yes, Mr. Cheung, Mooney could play the piano well. Let him show you.' She fleeted her eyes back and forth between Mooney and the birthday cake on the table: Mooney had got the plan. 'Sure,' he said, 'I'll play a piece by…Brahms.'

As Mooney's started to perform, all the guests in the house had their eyes fixed on him and were silenced. Charles, very much irritated, stood behind and watched. Not waiting until Mooney finished the piece, Charles yelled: 'Okay–it's time for my birthday cake!' Getting back all the attention, he ran to the table, lighted the candles and began to make a wish. He then picked up the knife beside him and sank it into the cake – as Sherlyn expected, several cockroaches squeezed out of the cake at the slice and fell on top of the table. In seconds, about fifty more of these creatures spilled out from the cake like beans from a basket, creeping all over the place like dark little ghosts. Everyone in the house was screaming on top of their voices and running around mad in circles, except for Mooney and his friends, of course, who limped out to the backyard laughing their legs off.

Coming out of nowhere, a butterfly glided through the air like a feather. 'The red butterfly!' Sherlyn exclaimed and immediately started to chase after it. 'Wait,' said Mooney, sitting down on the lawn playing with the grass.

'What are you waiting for?' cried Sherlyn. 'It's the red butterfly and–'

'Why do we have to follow it every time?' said Mooney.

'Oh–!' said Sherlyn. 'You want to see what happens if we don't follow it.'

'Yeah,' said Mooney. 'Then we'll know if it's really carrying a purpose of its own.'

So the three of them sat and waited. The red butterfly, having gone for some distance already, turned back to the backyard, lingered for a moment, and then flew again to the direction it was heading for. Noticing that the three of them didn't react, it came back again and circled hastily above their heads, but they still pretended to ignore it. Then the butterfly halted in front of Mooney, stared at him with its eyes and threw itself violently at his face, orbiting his head in madness. It was flying so fast that it looked like a fire that surrounded Mooney's

27

head, as it sprinkled his hair with shiny red powder. Sherlyn laughed and said, 'Mooney, I think you better give up now!' Then immediately the butterfly stopped spinning and turned for its destination again. Mooney, Sherlyn and Colin got up and chased after it.

Following the lead of the butterfly, the three went out of the house and finally reached the woods on the quieter side of Richmond. The trees there were very tall; once inside the place, the three felt like being totally separated from the outside world. 'It's too quiet in here,' whispered Sherlyn. 'It looks dangerous.'

'It's okay,' said Mooney. 'We all have special powers. And we won't give up until we get to where the butterfly stops, right?'

After another three minutes of walking, they heard some strange whisking sound coming from somewhere not far away from them. They saw the butterfly wings, whose colour stood out clearly among the green leaves, flying straight to where the sound was coming from.

Finally, the butterfly came to a stop on a tall oak tree. Mooney and his friends halted and saw an Asian boy, clad in gold and brown, turning a combination of summersaults in the air with incredible agility. In his hands there gripped a long stick, which twisted and twirled as his wrists wavered. His movements, like those of a dancer, seemed to follow a certain rhythm, and the stick in his hands was spinning so fast that it looked as if it had become invisible, that one could only see its shadow on the boy's robe. The whisking of the stick echoed with the boy's crisp howling, and the three visitors looked on and were amazed.

'It's Chinese Kung Fu!' said Mooney. 'I've seen it on TV – but this guy's at least a hundred times better than those people on TV!'

The boy stopped abruptly in the middle of his practice and looked at the three strangers with his big round eyes. Sherlyn and Colin took a step back behind Mooney and lowered their heads. Mooney noticed that the red butterfly had not disappeared yet; it flew to the three visitors, hovered awhile above their heads, and was gone then. The Asian boy smiled with great joy, threw his stick to the ground and ran to the visitors. 'Finally!' he cried. 'You've come – finally!'

The boy took off his hood and revealed his extremely short buzz-cut. He wasn't tall for a fourteen-year-old, but was well built, and it seemed to Sherlyn that he had the sweetest smile that reminded her of the bright morning. Rolling his big eyeballs, he seemed friendly and a little childish. He took Mooney's hand and said, 'Finally! I've waited two years for our meeting – and now, you've come!' Mooney was completely puzzled and didn't know what to say.

'Oh – is this too sudden?' said the boy. 'Sorry, I was being kind of rude, but do you guys not know about this?'

Sherlyn smiled and said, 'Hi, I'm Sherlyn. This is Mooney, and this is Colin. Have you been expecting us?'

'Of course!' said the boy. 'But I didn't know what your names are. Aren't you here to find me, though? Where – where is that red butterfly?'

As if it could understand what the boy just said, the red butterfly revealed itself again in the air. But this time it wasn't alone: there were four of them in total, all of them identical. They descended slowly among the four youngsters, who had now unconsciously formed a circle, seemingly to welcome the mysterious insects into their midst. Each of the four butterflies landed on the palms of the youngster, and lo! the butterflies started to glow, and as they slowly raised themselves into the air again, they shook off powder like golden stardust from their wings. The dust, now forming trails like silk ribbons, followed slowly behind the butterflies as they twisted up in spirals: crisscrossing in the air, the four golden trails now joined together to become a big halo, which lowered and surrounded the four youngsters. Involuntarily, the four of them joined their hands in a circle and closed their eyes; the halo then spun slowly around them, dimming gradually and at last to nothing.

Like newborns, the four youngsters opened their eyes, looked at each other and were glad. Their minds were clear as crystal, and they seemed to find each other's emotions deep inside their hearts.

'I'm not sure about what happened to us,' said Mooney, sitting on the floor of the woods. 'But we must find the answer, and we will.'

Sherlyn said slowly to the Asian boy, 'According to what you've said, it seems that you know something about this, right? Oh, we don't even know your name.'

'Oh, my bad,' said the boy. 'My name is Jing Neng. No, no…my real name is Wang Jun. Well, actually, you can just call me Jing.' Jing scratched his head and picked up his stick from the ground. He disassembled it into three equal parts and put it into the red silk casing on his back. 'I know just a little about the matter,' he continued. 'I don't know if I can help.'

'Tell us what you know,' said Sherlyn.

'I don't know anything about the purpose behind this matter,' said Jing, 'but I'll tell you everything. My real name is Wang Jun, and my parents stowed away on a ship from China to Canada when I was one year old, leaving me behind in China with my grandpa. Later, my grandpa decided to send me to the Shaolin Temple, and so I went.

'After I became a monk in the Temple, my master gave me a new name called Jing Neng. Jing means "silence" or "serenity at heart," and Neng means "to be able." Anyway, I learned Kung Fu very fast; I came in first in the national championship when I was six, and my master gave me this stick as a reward. He said I am a genius or something, and that the Temple hasn't seen a fighter like me in the past few hundred years.

'So, I stayed at the Temple and learned to become a real combat fighter with my stick. Until two years ago, my parents became legal

The Mission of Mooney Rooney

immigrants in Canada, and they posted me a mail telling me to come and live with them. I didn't want to leave Shaolin, of course, and my master didn't want me to leave either. But after two months, a lama came to Shaolin from Tibet; there was a huge welcome for him and his escort. I heard that lamas were rulers in Tibet, and that this high lama was their leader. This lama went inside a room to see the Shaolin Grandmaster, and later, someone told me to go inside that room. I went in, and saw the two great figures waiting for me – I was so scared that I nearly fell to the floor.

'That lama smiled at me – he seemed very friendly. He waved his hand and told me to come near him; and I did. He held my hands, and I felt a stream of warmth coming from his palm and slowly up to my chest. It was really comfortable. Then he released me, turning to the Grandmaster and said, "This is the one." And the Grandmaster said to me: "This old father has something to tell you. Remember it well." I nodded.

' "My son," said the lama, "there are many things in the world that you still don't understand. But there's something here that concerns the future of the world. Although your power is limited, you would still do your best if I ask, would you?" I nodded again. "You don't have to ask why," he continued. "Just listen and obey what I say. I know that you are still thinking of staying in the Temple, but now I tell you that you must go to Canada. There should be three people waiting for you."

' "You mean my...my parents?" I asked.

' "No," he answered. "You haven't met these people before. But don't worry – they'll come to you. Remember: the red butterfly."

' "What red butterfly?" I asked.

' "You don't need to ask too many questions, my son. Remember: after you have met these three people, go and find the Black Sphere. By that time, you will know everything you will need to know."

'So, I came to Canada and waited for you everyday. And now, finally, you've come.'

Mooney, Sherlyn and Colin looked at each other and could utter no word for several minutes. But finally Sherlyn spoke. 'So, according to your story, Jing, there is some sort of agenda behind our meeting. But who would've been planned this all? The lama?'

'That is not the most important thing at hand,' said Mooney. 'It is — '

'The Black Sphere!' cried Sherlyn. 'We'll find the answer once we find the Black Sphere. But what is it? Where — '

'Well I do have some idea of that,' said Jing. 'After I got here, I've been reading the news everyday trying to improve my English. A few months ago, I came across some reports about the appearance of a mysterious black sphere in Las Vegas, and I suspected that it is the one we are looking for. I gathered some information about that thing – let's go to my house and look at it together.'

Mooney and Sherlyn hesitated. Everything had come too suddenly, and they wondered if it was nothing but a dream. 'Oh god!' cried Mooney. 'What time is it? My parents are still at the party! We should hurry back – Jing, we'll come to your house, maybe in a few days.'

Chapter 6
The Long Journey

Mooney and Sherlyn were troubled at heart. They were still dazed about the story Jing had told them, wishing that it wasn't true. They didn't know why they should trust Jing, but it seemed to them that they have been friends for years, and they had got to trust him. What was it that they were going to face? Should they really go for it? Despite their special powers, they were kids after all, and they couldn't shake off the thought that the matter "concerned the future of the world" as the mysterious lama had told Jing. How were they going to explain it to their parents, or were they going to tell them at all?

Today, the four friends were at Jing's house.

Jing's parents had gone to work early in the morning. Since becoming legal workers, they had been working even harder than before, and they usually came home late at night. Because of this, the family hadn't been spending much time together. Due to the fact that Jing was having trouble with his English when he first arrived, his parents hired a private tutor who came to his house every day, helping him overcome the language barrier. And since Jing took every opportunity to speak and learn English, he improved so quickly that already he sounded like a natural speaker. Nonetheless, he was still making some grammatical errors in his composition for school.

Now the four of them were sitting around a table, looking at the newspaper cut-outs that Jing had gathered. What they saw were some pictures and articles on the discovery of the Black Sphere but nothing of a detailed description or analysis. They hadn't got a clue of how this piece of news could be linked with themselves.

'Why don't we just travel to Las Vegas,' said Colin, who hadn't been participating in the investigation.

'But it's Las Vegas!' said Jing. 'It's too far away – how are we going to get there?'

'That is a problem actually,' said Mooney. 'If we are really going there, we have to leave home, and we need money, passport, everything…it's kind of troublesome.'

Knowing that the future was moving close and plans becoming real, the youngsters hesitated. They still doubted the necessity of their effort in the participation in the "matter."

'Where is Las Vegas?' said Colin abruptly.

'It's in the state of Nevada in America,' said Mooney. 'It takes about two hours to fly there from Vancouver. I've been there once with my dad.'

'We can go there by Reddash,' said Colin. 'It's even faster than an airplane.'

'Are you kidding?' cried Mooney and Sherlyn together. 'Going to America on that cloth?'

'What, "radish"?' asked Jing. 'What cloth?'

So Mooney told Jing about Colin's cloth. 'Well,' said Jing, 'I don't really trust that thing either, just by hearing you say. I don't think it could fly that far. We could well be falling off from it too.'

34

The Mission of Mooney Rooney

'You don't trust me,' grumbled Colin. 'You two have been on Reddash and you still don't trust me!' And he turned his back against them.

'Colin, we didn't mean that,' said Sherlyn. 'But in order to get to Nevada, we have to cross the Cascade Mountains. Isn't that too dangerous if we–'

'I don't care about what Cascade Mountains,' said Colin. 'All I know is that my Reddash hasn't failed me before. Anyway, it's up to you if you want to use it.'

'Well then,' said Mooney. 'I think we could give it a try, since it's the fastest way possible. But we have to figure out the route first. Colin, are you sure we won't fall off Reddash?' All he got from Colin was a childish glare.

'Okay. Now we should get a map and a compass,' said Mooney. 'Once we've found the direction, it's not hard for us to get to the Black Sphere. And if we can't find it we can always come back.' On the table, Mooney spread out the map that Jing handed to him. 'Colin, how long does it take going from here to there? Half a day?'

'Much less than that,' said Colin.

'It's that fast?' said Jing. 'Man, I don't believe that.'

'Well,' said Mooney, 'should we go home and start packing up a bit now? We need things like clothes and food – it's going to be freezing up there in the air.'

'Sure,' said Sherlyn, smiling.

So they left Jing and went home to get ready for the journey.

* * *

Today, the four of them were at Mooney's backyard. Each carrying a backpack, they were all ready to take off. Colin took out Reddash and climbed onto it.

'That's amazing!' cried Jing. 'That's amazing!'

'Hang on to the margins of the cloth,' said Colin, 'and imagine that you're one with it.' And at Colin's finger signal, Reddash left the backyard in a second and found itself among the clouds.

Despite that they were travelling at a high speed up in the air, they didn't seem to stumble or have any problem breathing. Mooney and Sherlyn had thrown away all their doubts about the cloth, but Jing was too scared to look down – it was his first ride after all. He grabbed Mooney by his shoulder and hid his head behind it, and everyone laughed.

After confirming the direction on Jing's map, the four of them slowly began to enjoy their trip. After ten minutes or so, Jing took his first look down on the Cascade Mountains below and was astonished. Neither Mooney nor Sherlyn had been so close to the snowy caps of the Mountains. Sometimes they slowed down and flew low in the valleys, feeding birds that flew by their sides. They laughed and ate, and it was summertime.

'We're almost there!' said Colin. Since they didn't know the exact location of the Sphere, they had to hover above the Las Vegas area for about twenty minutes before they spotted it. Just as it was described on the news, the Black Sphere was withheld inside the great Light Pillar stretching vertically from the sky to the ground. 'We found it! We found it!' cried Sherlyn. But Mooney saw a small troop of military police guarding near the pillar. 'It's not the right time to go forward now,' he said. 'Let's wait first.'

'What?' said Jing. 'What if the guards won't go away? We can't be waiting like this the whole day.'

'We still got some food,' said Sherlyn. 'We can have a little snack in the air. How's that?'

'Oh that's a perfect idea,' said Jing. He immediately took out a sandwich from his backpack and started eating again.

36

The Mission of Mooney Rooney

Mooney looked at the Pillar of Light and muttered, 'How are we going to reach the Sphere? According to the information we got, people can't get any close to the Pillar.'

'We can fly over to it and have a look,' said Colin.

'No,' said Mooney, 'it's too obvious. The police will see us. The Sphere is only about a hundred feet above the ground.'

'Wait till it's dark then,' said Sherlyn.

'Till it's dark?' cried Jing. 'It's only two o'clock in the afternoon!'

'We can find a place to rest and then come back at night,' said Sherlyn.

'No,' groaned Jing. 'We said we'll take a look at the thing quick and then go home – I haven't told my parents about it...and I've got to go home!'

Sherlyn thought for a bit and said, 'Okay then. We can fly over real fast, and people won't notice.'

So they speeded toward the Pillar of Light. As expected, they felt a force coming towards them as they moved near the Pillar. As well, the light from the Pillar was so strong that they had to shut their eyes tight and to back off a little. Mooney struggled to unlock his eyelids, and saw a huge, solemn black sphere floating in front of him.

Suddenly he heard someone crying, 'Hey, what's that red thing up there?'

'Yinks,' said Sherlyn, still struggling against the force from the Pillar. 'They saw us. Let's go!'

'No, Wait!' cried Mooney. 'There's something down there–!' In the midst of blinding light, Mooney saw that a deep black hole appeared at the bottom of the Sphere, and was expanding gradually. However Colin heard the sound of two helicopters coming near them; like a flash, Reddash lurched away from the pillar and vanished behind a hill.

'Oh man...' groaned Jing, 'let's go home...'

37

'No, we can't,' said Mooney. 'We can't give up until we find the mystery of the Sphere.' He glanced at his three friends, who were at once filled with spirit again. 'Okay,' said Jing. 'We're staying. But what are we going to do now?'

'It's impossible for us to go near the Pillar the way we just did,' said Sherlyn. 'I think we should wait until it gets darker, and try to walk near it and see if there's any opening at its bottom.'

'Yeah,' said Colin; 'I certainly hated the heat.'

'Heat?' said Mooney. 'I didn't feel any heat. Wasn't there only light from the Pillar?'

'You couldn't feel any heat?' said Sherlyn. 'That's strange...well, we'll wait for a miracle tonight.'

*   *   *

The Pillar research team leader Dr. Ince was informed about the red object that appeared in the afternoon. But since the object was never found again after it was gone, Dr. Ince and his team took no further action regarding its appearance.

Now the sun had just sunk into the west. 'It's time,' said Mooney. The four of them then flew slowly from behind the hill and landed near one of the patrol camps. After Colin has put away Reddash, the four of them tiptoed toward the Pillar. When they were about to reach it, the light from it shone on them, and their long shadows were seen by the guards. 'Hey, you four! What are you doing here?' And at once the four of them were surrounded by armed police. Now Jing had already pulled out his stick from the casing on his back, swiftly snapped the three parts together and begun his moves. 'Hide behind me!' he cried to his friends. 'This is called the "Ba Gua Trick" – watch me!'

Spinning incredibly fast, the stick formed a glowing shield around the four youngsters, parrying every policeman who tried to move near.

38

The Mission of Mooney Rooney

But one fierce guard stepped out and said, 'Put your weapon down! Or else I'll sh–' He swallowed the last word of his sentence, for he saw that they were just kids. So the four of them hid behind the "Ba Gua Shield," until finally, Dr. Ince showed up among the crowd. 'What are you doing here, little ones?' he said slowly. 'It's too dangerous around here – come to my office and we'll talk.'

At this moment, Mooney suddenly turned to his back and walked slowly toward the Pillar. 'No!' cried Dr. Ince. 'Come back! Don't go there! My office is this way…' He stepped forward trying to pull Mooney back, but Jing's "Ba Gua Shield" was in his way. He had no choice but to stand there in frustration.

Mooney's mind was now blank. Reaching the bottom of the Pillar, the redhead continued to move forward. He strode through the heat field, and slowly, in the sight of many, his body entered the Pillar of Light. Opening up his arms, he ascended slowly up the Pillar and traveled toward the Black Sphere. Finally, as he reached the bottom of the Sphere, his entire body seemed to gleam white. It was absorbed into the Black Sphere and was gone.

Loosening the "Ba Gua Shield," Sherlyn, Colin and Jing stood hand in hand looking up at the Sphere. Together they waited, in hope and faith, that Mooney was going to return safe with tidings of joy, relief, or peace. Dr. Ince scratched his half-bald head and was in thought. He was a science genius despite his looks, and he knew that there were many things in the world that even the wisest men could not explain. And now, right in front of him, there stood one of the many things that were certainly beyond the reach of science.

Minutes went by, and they seemed like years to those who waited. The Black Sphere stirred, finally, and emitted white, eye-piercing light rays. As the rays diminished, the Black Sphere disappeared, and Mooney's body descended slowly through the Pillar of Light, which also ceased to exist after he reached the ground. As if coming back from a battle, Mooney stumbled and wavered before Sherlyn, Jing and Colin, who ran to him and saw that the light of his eyes was spent, and that he was weary and pale like a piece of paper. Dr. Ince knew that this matter wasn't simple, and he clutched the children by their shoulders and said, 'Come to my office. We won't be talking for a while, until you've had enough rest.' Then he turned to the police and said, 'Tell absolutely no one about what happened today. And do not come in without my order.' And he slammed the door of his office.

Chapter 7

The Mission of Mooney

Although Dr. Ince's office looked plain and small, there sat countless equipments of high technology neatly in place. Dr. Ince gave the kids four glasses of water and let them rest on the chairs around the table in the center of the room.

'Where are you from?' asked Dr. Ince kindly. 'What are you trying to do here?'

'Didn't you see it a while ago already?' said Sherlyn. 'And who are you – why do we need to tell you anything?'

Much to Sherlyn's surprise, Colin burst into laughing. In fact, He had wanted to laugh in the first place, when he saw Dr. Ince's fat body squeezing among the crowd of police with much difficulty. 'What are you laughing at?' said the poor scientist. 'You seem to be the youngest here, and yet you have the courage to come and see the Pillar. Anyhow, can you tell me why you have come?' Colin looked at Mooney, but Mooney was gazing down at the table and didn't seem to have heard their conversation. Sherlyn went over to Mooney and whispered, 'It's okay. We're going home.'

But Mooney lifted up his head and said to Dr. Ince, 'Sir, I believe that you are a powerful man, and I think I'd be going to need your

41

help. But can you promise that you are going to do your best, no matter what?'

Dr. Ince was a trusting person, and Mooney knew that he could rely on him. 'Okay,' said Dr. Ince. 'My name is Ince, and I'm the research team leader, commander of the whole national squad concerning the tornado. Well, I'm not the President of the United States, but I always do my best at everything. I'm a scientist, and I believe in all the queerest things in the world. So, tell me about it: what can I do to help?'

'Hey wait – you got anything to eat?' said Jing.

'Of course,' said Dr. Ince, smiling.

*   *   *

So this is what happened...

As Mooney was walking to the Pillar, he heard a voice talking to him. He didn't hear it through his ears; it seemed to have come straight to his brain from nowhere. At first, the voice sounded like an order, a sort of command, and Mooney's body obeyed it involuntarily. As he entered the Pillar, he felt a strong force pulling him upwards and into the Black Sphere.

He opened his eyes, but all he could see was nothing but whiteness all around him. He felt that his feet were touching the floor. 'Pay attention to the screen,' said the voice told, and at once the white space turned into something like a visual theatre. At first, the screen went black, and he saw a 3D image of a mass of stars that twirled like a giant whirlpool. Then, the view zoomed in, focusing on a single planet, which, spinning ceaselessly, shot out a shaft of light which directed to another planet far away. Along the shaft, numerous tiny particles like dust (Mooney couldn't see them clearly) traveled from the original planet to the other. When all the "particles" had reached

42

The Mission of Mooney Rooney

the second planet, the shaft disappeared, and suddenly the original planet exploded. The focus then turned to the second planet, and on top of the screen above Mooney's head there appeared three smaller insert screens. At first, the inserts altogether showed images of a single environment. But after a while, this environment developed into three distinctive worlds, represented in the three insert screens respectively. Mooney was shocked to see that one of these worlds was exactly the same as the one he was living in. One of the other two developed into a plain, clear, beautiful environment, and the other turned into a strange, dark, and gloomy world. Then the voice said, 'Now, you've seen it all. But do not be surprised! These three worlds all originated from Earth, and they co-exist in different spaces or dimensions called Partitions. The Immigrants were distributed into the Three Partitions on Earth by pure chance following the Great Travel, but because of the different environments, the Three Peoples evolved differently to adapt to their own Worlds...'

'Do I, then, exist in one of the Worlds?' asked Mooney. But the voice didn't answer him; it seemed like a tape that lectured only to itself.

It continued: 'In the first place, the Three Worlds didn't know of the existence of one another. However, because of the openings called Leap Holes that are found between the Partitions, the Worlds got to know of each other's existence, though obscurely, through time. Respectively, the Three Worlds are named Aetheria, Valeor, and Ündia. Because Valeor's evolution progress is rather slow, the Valeorans fear and know little about the other two Worlds. In fact, there's nothing for them to fear, because the Worlds were created equal...'

'To which World do I belong?' asked Mooney. 'And who are you?' But there was no answer.

'Later,' said the voice, 'the leader of Ündia became strong in power, and was ambitious to rule the Three Worlds: he began his attack in Valeor. He invaded the weak minds of the Valeorans, causing them to kill one another. In order to stop the Ündian attack, Aetheria called upon the Emissary of the Universe, who lived in another planet. The Emissary appeared in Valeor and attempted to restore the balance between the Three Worlds. However, as the Emissary was about to accomplish His task, something happened in His home planet, forcing Him to abandon everything on Earth. Before He left, He sealed up most of the Leap Holes between Ündia and Valeor, where He has also planted the Seeds. He created markings in various places in Valeor, in order to prevent future Ündian attacks. When these markings are corrupted or destroyed, they will send out a signal for the Emissary's return.

'After the Emissary left, Valeor has gained peace for a long while. However, Ündia hasn't given up. In the past century, the force of Ündia has emerged again in Valeor. The Ündians have apparently grown even stronger, and the markings set by the Emissary can no longer hold them,' the voice trembled with fear. 'And, most unfortunately, we've found out that a few thousand years ago, the Ündians had already destroyed the device that calls for the return of the Emissary ...'

The voice suddenly stopped, as if giving Mooney some time to think and digest the story. And it continued: 'Mooney...'

Mooney nearly fell to the floor upon hearing his own name. 'Now Valeor is in danger. For peace, you and your three friends are destined to take up the mission of restoring peace on Earth. Remember: this mission is full of toils and perils, and that you should be prepared to lose your lives once you have decided on taking up the responsibility. Yes, you have a choice; but once you have made your decision, you cannot go back. If you choose to fulfill your destiny, you must now go and find

The Mission of Mooney Rooney

the Rainbow Bridge, where you will enter Aetheria. Farewell! I hope that I will see you someday. Farewell!'

'Wait!' cried Mooney. 'Where's Rainbow Bridge? When does our mission start? What is it? How–' But all he could hear was the echoes of his own voice.

Like falling into a dream, Mooney faintly saw something glittering around him. They were small birds and butterflies, thought Mooney, and they rejoiced, flying among high clouds, through mountains and over waters – living freely in a world like paradise. Abruptly, a strong light shone on him, and when he could see again, all was the faces of Sherlyn, Jing, and Colin.

* * *

There was a silence for a long while in Dr. Ince's office. Indeed, how ridiculous this story was! Everybody in the office seemed to have lost the ability to think; everything had lost its order, and the world was logical no longer...

'Sherlyn,' said Colin all of sudden. 'I'm tired. I want to go to bed.'

'That's actually a good idea,' said Dr. Ince with a weak voice. 'If we still remember what happened tonight when we wake up the next morning, then this is not a dream, and we have to make plans, and please, let me contact your parents – I'll know what to say.'

Dr. Ince called in several guards and told them to lead the children to a place where they could rest. After they had left, Dr. Ince sat beside the phone, now picking it up, now putting it down: he had never come across such a situation in his entire life, and his heart was heavy.

Chapter 8
The Guide

'It's too much for me,' said Dr. Ince, giving up his half-eaten breakfast the next morning.

'I can finish the rest for you, Mr. Chubby,' said Jing.

Everyone remembered what happened last night. The secret of the Black Sphere was revealed, finally, but it was too hard for anyone to believe a thing like that. Looking at the four children, Dr. Ince was filled with pity. They were too young – far too young – to face such a ridiculous destiny, if there was really one intended for them.

'Hey Mr. Chubby, did you phone our parents last night?' asked Jing, finishing his glass of milk.

'That doesn't matter anymore,' said Sherlyn. 'We can't always be thinking about ourselves now. All that matters is the World and its people.'

'They say you have a choice,' said Dr. Ince, 'whether you want to go or not. I'm really worried about you all – how am I going to speak with your parents in case you–'

'Who cares?' said Colin, chewing and staring down at the bread in his hand. 'Everyone dies sooner or later, and is forgotten then.'

46

The Mission of Mooney Rooney

Finally Mooney said, 'What Sherlyn said is right. We have to learn not to put ourselves on top of everything else. But now I am wondering: who is the owner of the voice that spoke to me? I think he's on the side of "Aetheria," but he could be a trap for us, since I think what he said was a little biased. What do you think, Colin?'

But Colin stood up and buried his head into Dr. Ince's belly. 'I haven't had a hug with my dad for a very long time, Mr. Chubby,' he said. 'But you see, grownups are too complicated. Everything is better when it is simple, just like kids. Why can't we just do as the voice has told us, and who cares if we make mistakes? Who is to judge right and wrong?'

'That's right!' shouted Jing. 'Just do it!'

Dr. Ince was silenced. He was a grownup, and he seemed to worry the most about everything. He thought for a bit, and said, 'Now I think I should tell you something – don't know if it would be of any help. After the Black Sphere has appeared here in North America, there were reports about the respective occurrences of six unnatural things in the remaining six continents. According to the reports, these six things were very similar to the Black Sphere we had here, and the governments could do nothing about them. Recently, some of these unnatural things disappeared mysteriously in the other continents, and I guess ours disappeared last night, didn't it. Well, therefore, I conclude that you are not alone.'

'Well that's good news,' said Mooney. 'Anyway Mr. Chubby, if we aren't going to come back for a while, will you manage to explain to our parents?'

But Sherlyn interrupted, 'Where is Rainbow Bridge? I'm so excited for the trip.'

'There is a natural stone bridge in southern Utah,' said Dr. Ince. 'It's called "Rainbow Bridge" by the natives there, who say that the bridge

47

changes colour when the sun shines on it. But I am not sure if that is the one.'

'Probably,' said Mooney. 'But where exactly in Utah is it? How are we going to find it?'

'That's not a problem in fact,' said Dr. Ince. 'I'll take you there.'

'When should we be leaving?' asked Sherlyn.

'I don't know,' said Mooney. 'The voice didn't say.'

'I guess that means we should be going as soon as possible,' said Colin.

'So what are we waiting for?' said Jing. 'Let's go!'

* * *

The Rainbow Bridge was considered sacred among the American Natives, especially the Navajo Nation. Being part of the canyon that engulfed Lake Powell, it was among the largest natural bridges in the world.

'We can't get too close to it,' said Dr. Ince on his administrative cruiser boat on Lake Powell. 'It's an inhibited area over there. But I can arrange a helicopter ride for you if you want.'

'There's no need,' said Sherlyn. 'We have our own way. There are too many tourists here…um, can you arrange hotel rooms for us? We'll come back tomorrow morning.'

'Sure,' said Dr. Ince. 'But you have to tell me how you are going to approach the Bridge.'

'No problem,' said Sherlyn. 'Come with us before we leave tomorrow morning, and you'll see.'

The five of them got up before sunrise the next morning and had breakfast in the hotel where they stayed. Then they went to the small hill behind the hotel and got ready for flight. Colin took out Reddash and showed it to Dr. Ince, who hugged the four children one by one before

48

they climbed onto the cloth. 'Do come back!' said Dr. Ince, holding his tears and smiling.

'No worries, Mr. Chubby,' said Mooney. 'We'll be back.' And Reddash took off.

Since they had already been near the Bridge, they had no problem locating it. Now the sun had just risen, and the Bridge displayed its beautiful colours across the lake. While Reddash was hovering in the air and the children staring at the Bridge, there suddenly appeared a dark cloud in the corner of the sky, looking like a huge, black piece of clay from far away.

'That cloud looks a bit strange' cried Jing. 'It seems to be…moving. Is it coming at us?'

The cloud was already fifty yards away, when they realized that it was actually not a cloud. 'Oh my!' cried Sherlyn. 'It's locusts!' But it was too late. The cloud of locusts engulfed them like a whale, knocking the four of them out of Reddash. As they were falling through the air, the black-headed locusts bit them on their heads and legs with powerful jaws and cut their skins with the sharp edges of their wings. Sherlyn, struggling from pain, landed on a floor of flying locusts with the tip of her right foot and sprang to the falling Colin above her. Grabbing the boy by her right hand, she vaguely saw that Jing, who wouldn't stop cursing and swinging his stick, was falling right below her. 'Hand me that fighting stick!' she cried. Despite all the horror and pain, Jing reached out his stick as far as he could and let Sherlyn get hold of its end. Again, Sherlyn tipped her toe on one the locusts and jumped up to Reddash; with great difficulty, the three of them climbed back onto the cloth and flew out of the cloud of insects. 'Go get Mooney – quick! He's in the lake!' At once Reddash hurried down to Mooney, whose legs kicked violently underwater, and arms waved helplessly against the attack of the locusts from above his head. Jing quickly reached his stick into the water and tossed it up with great precision – Mooney was launched out of the lake like a rocket, and Reddash received him as he fell.

Speeding, they turned and saw that the black cloud was still chasing madly after them. 'Into the water!' cried Sherlyn, and at once the four of them held their breath and dived like a small meteor into Lake Powell with Reddash. Underwater, they heard loud thudding sounds as the insects knocked their bodies violently onto the surface of the lake and smashed themselves into pastes as they drowned. When Reddash emerged out of the water, the four youngsters looked down and saw a huge, black mass floating on the lake. It was horrid.

'Aw man!' moaned Jing. 'They really hurt!'

'But Mooney, why didn't you tell those locusts to go away?' asked Sherlyn.

'I couldn't,' said Mooney. 'They were like the red butterfly – I couldn't communicate with them at all. I don't think they are normal. Anyway, let's try flying to the Bridge again.'

'Now what on earth is going on?' said Jing, who turned and saw that there wasn't only one Bridge before them – there were at least twenty identical bridges shining in rainbow colours under the sun!

'It's illusions,' said Sherlyn. 'Someone's trying to trick us.'

But Colin smiled and said, 'We shouldn't be looking at them then.'

'You're right,' said Mooney. 'We'll use our internal feelings instead of senses.'

Hand in hand, the four of them closed their eyes. Their minds became clear. Then Mooney heard a calling, and he cried, 'Now!' And at once Reddash flew and vanished under the Rainbow Bridge.

* * *

The Mission of Mooney Rooney

All turned white around them. As they gazed into the midst of nothingness, they saw a tiny, bright spot of light, and Reddash moved slowly towards it. Gradually the whiteness faded, and an unseen world came into life: the four youngsters looked around them, and saw that the sky above was blue like the clearest sapphire, and that the land below was covered by unknown, giant green plants and gorgeous tiny flowers. There were no buildings of any sort; it was a completely natural world, like an ancient jungle. Yet, it was more peaceful and comforting, and there were many strokes of pastel-coloured mists that crept silently through the air. 'Are we in heaven?' said Sherlyn.

'If we are, then we must be dead,' said Jing.

'If we really died,' said Mooney smiling, 'then things would be better for us, since now we wouldn't have to die again. Well, this is probably "Aetheria." '

Suddenly, a silver light flashed in front of them before a figure appeared. The face of this figure was engraved with age, and his ears were small like peas. He had no facial hair, but the hair on his head was long and was floating in the air like thousands of little moving snakes. Clad all in white and wearing no shoes, the figure stood on a small white cloud that supported him in the air.

'You're not an angel, are you?' said Sherlyn. 'Angels have wings, and they are young and beautiful.'

But the figure smiled kindly and said, 'My name is Muloka Jibrelle, your guide. I've been waiting here for very long.' He twitched his right hand a little and abruptly the youngster's bodies were dried. He pointed at Reddash and said, 'You don't need this for now; ride on these!' As he stretched out both of his arms and drew a big circle in the air, some of the wandering mists of different pastel colours gathered slowly in front of his chest. He now held the mists in his palms, then released them: like magic, four nameless, giant birds were revealed howling right in front of the kids, who stood without a word on top of Reddash. 'Here, you have come dead,' said Muloka, smiling, 'and you will not die again. Now follow me!'

But Mooney laughed. 'Don't you worry – we fear nothing. Let's go!'

The four of them jumped onto the birds and followed Muloka. Muloka's cloud glided through the air like a bullet, and his feet didn't have to move at all. After Colin had put away Reddash, the five of them travelled swiftly and eagerly across the sky of Aetheria.

Chapter 9
Aetheria

Riding comfortably on his bird, Mooney looked down to the quiet world below and saw creeks and meadows lying undisturbed on the floors of Aetheria while clouds stirred high in the sky beneath the gentle sun. In fact, other than the four giant birds, Mooney could see no moving life-forms or "animals" around him, save a few beings in the likes of Muloka that glided pass the youngsters, if they were "animals" at all.

Now the five of them had slowed down and come before a great mountain, where plants were scarcely seen. They flew along the line of extremely steep slopes and finally halted in front of a vertical, smooth rock surface. This strange surface was as large as an acre, giving out wavelike illusions that made the four youngsters uneasy. But as Muloka was standing on his cloud in front of the rock surface, every single strand of his white hair trembled as if he was given a mild electric shock. 'You can go in now,' he said.

Sherlyn ran her hands down nervously on her ponytail. 'I think you should explain this to us before we go in.'

But Muloka smiled and said, 'There's no hurry. Go in first and I'll tell you.'

The four youngsters shut their eyes as their birds dived into the rock one by one. But when they opened their eyes again, they looked below them, and they saw a gigantic, civilized place like a city that knew no bound. There were numerous grey-coloured buildings that sat neatly across the landscape, but the youngsters were just too high up to look at them in detail.

'Oh, I get it now,' said Sherlyn. 'You live here inside this mountain, not anywhere outside. Is this a city?'

'A city?' said Muloka. 'Ah, yes. There are actually many of these cities all across Aetheria, and yes, we do live in them. We seldom go outside, unless we have to travel to other cities.'

'Do you all fly?' asked Jing.

'Well,' said Muloka, "all of the grownups do."

The five of them then flew toward the centre of the city, where buildings were of basic shapes and similar sizes. These buildings were sorted and grouped together according to their shapes, with the taller ones standing out among the others. Now that the five of them had landed on a spacious street, the cloud under Muloka's feet disappeared. At a fling of his arm, the giant birds turned back into four puffs of Wandering Mists, which looked thicker and smaller than it does outside the city. Sparingly, beings in the likes of Muloka walked on the open street with bare feet and in white robes, some standing on slowly flying clouds. Every time as the beings met, their hair quivered in the air; as soon as they parted, their hair turned back to the normal floating state.

'That looks interesting,' said Colin. 'Do you talk with your hair?'

'You are very clever,' said Muloka. 'We have already developed the ability to exchange brainwaves via our hair strands, and we don't have to speak anymore. But now, for your convenience, I have implanted a language chip inside myself, so that I can speak in any language with

54

you. Look at my ears – they have shrunk a lot already.' He bent his head and let Colin touch his pea-like ears that looked like small faces.

Taking a closer look, Mooney saw that the buildings in the city were all made out of the same greyish white material that he was sure none could be found in his World. Also, instead of windows, the buildings had large circular holes on their walls that formed strange patterns. No trees or shrubs could be found anywhere on the streets.

'Where are we going, Muloka?' asked Sherlyn.

'We are going to meet the commander of your mission,' said Muloka.

'Is that the mission Mooney has spoken of?' asked Sherlyn.

'Yes, but what Mooney knows is only an introduction,' said Muloka. 'You are here to learn the details.'

As they continued to walk, they saw several beings that looked like small children, who flew by their sides and surveyed them from head to toe. Clad all in white, these children-like beings had a pair of feathered wings on their back. 'It's angels!' Sherlyn shouted.

'All of our children are produced by our Leaders,' said Muloka. 'They have no parents. They were born with wings, which will drop until they have learned all their skills...'

'What?' said Jing. 'They were "produced" by your Leaders? You mean artificially?'

'Yes, but they're real beings like you and me,' said Muloka. 'We've been doing this for a very long time in order to control population. Isn't Valeor trying to do the same now?'

'What do you mean?' said Colin. 'Too bad those children don't have parents to love them.'

'What? Love?' said Muloka. 'Oh...! That thing! Well, I do know what it is, but I don't think it exists anymore here in Aetheria – perhaps

it did, in ancient times. Why, is love a very important thing in Valeor?'
Colin lowered his head and didn't answer.

'You know,' said Sherlyn, 'perhaps who we refer to as "angels" are in fact the Aetherian children.'

'Probably,' said Muloka. 'Some people in your World might have dropped into Leap Holes accidentally and come to Aetheria. A very small number of them might have found their way back to Valeor and told the others about what they saw. I know that somehow, Aetheria has become what is known to you as "heaven" or "paradise" or "dreamland," et cetera.'

But the youngsters were confused. 'Could you please explain that to us a bit more clearly?' asked Sherlyn.

'Sure,' Muloka laughed. 'I understand that you have a lot of questions being here in a foreign place. But there's no hurry: I will explain that to you again until you have met the commander of your mission.'

'But could you just answer this question real quick: how…how do you "produce" your children?' asked Mooney.

'Well,' answered Muloka, 'all of the animals here are produced. They were formed by the gathering of the Wandering Mists in the atmosphere, which are actually disassembled chromosomes mixed with other important organic materials. Since little, we Aetherians have been learning how to utilize the Mists and recycle them.'

'And that means you create people using the Mists?' asked Mooney.

'Well, creating people is a little bit different from that,' said Muloka. 'We need things that resemble wombs to nourish our babies. We use machines.'

Jing laughed. 'That's interesting,' he said. 'And you know, those giant birds we rode today were really cool – I haven't seen them before in our World.'

The Mission of Mooney Rooney

'In fact, many of the animals in Aetheria are extinct,' said Muloka. 'Only those of good quality are left behind.'

'Wow, then what do you do if you're hungry?' asked Jing.

'We're vegetarians,' said Muloka. 'We never ate meat. The Immigrants never ate meat.'

Jing gave out an awkward smile. 'Is it against the rules if you make me some beef right now?' he said. 'I'm really hungry.'

They had come to a stop in front of a tall building that looked like a castle. This building was constructed with enormous rough rocks that were slightly flattened and stacked with the smaller ones at the bottom and the larger ones on the top. The five of them entered the first level of the castle and walked toward the end of the hall, where everything, including the floor and the pillars on the sides, was greyish white in colour. Even the faces of the guards who stood by the pillars looked solemn and emotionless.

'I've wished that one day I could go to "heaven,"' said Jing, 'but now I've changed my mind.'

'O, why so?' said Muloka. 'We have no desire here, and we don't fight for anything – isn't that ideal?'

'Sometimes when things are too ideal, they become nothing,' said Jing. 'Plus, you don't even love. There's nothing exciting here.'

'Our evolution is totally different from yours,' said Muloka. 'People in Valeor sought excitement in their lives; but is pleasure really necessary in life?'

Coming to the end of the hall, they saw a white chair on top of a platform elevated by some stairs. Then, an Aetherian man came out from behind the platform with a small escort, seating himself on the white chair. This man was wearing a pale golden robe, and his white hair floated slowly in the air above his grim face. Now Muloka took a step forward and said, 'Master, here is another group of youngsters.

57

They're Mooney, Sherlyn, Jing, and Colin.' He didn't use his hair to talk, probably because of the youngsters' presence.

'Very well,' said the Master with a clear and powerful voice. 'First of all, welcome to Aetheria. I'm the commander of your mission, and am here to instruct and prepare you for it. We have done our best with our technology in sending the seven Black Spheres to Valeor. We put the Spheres in each of the seven continents, since we are to summon seven groups of youngsters, including you.

'One of the most important land-markings that signal for the return of the Emissary is the Stonehenge in Valeor, which was complete with all its Hengestones when it was made. The correct placement of the Stones held a balancing force within the land-marking, and if we position the spirit of the Emissary, which is held inside the Sacred Jewel, at the centre of the Stonehenge, the land-marking will send out a signal to outer space, calling for the Emissary. However, about a thousand years ago, Ündia started to invade Valeor again. They had become stronger, and they stole seven of the most important Hengestones from the land-marking and hid them. Aetheria's power is limited, and we need you to help uncover the lost Hengestones, for the sake of the whole planet.'

'But who are we to do anything,' said Sherlyn, 'when even your power is limited?'

'You are the Seeds that the Emissary Himself had planted before He left our planet,' said the Master. 'Perhaps He has already foreseen the coming of this day. Now, you have grown up to be His Seedlings, all carrying special powers and the ability to travel freely between the three Partitions – it is all recorded on the secret scheme designed by the Emissary. But you are not powerful enough to fight the Ündians just yet, so you must stay here and attend the training we've planned for you.'

The Mission of Mooney Rooney

'How likely are we going to succeed?' asked Sherlyn. 'What will happen to us if we fail to find the Hengestones? Are we all going to die in the hands of Ündia?' But the Master didn't answer. Sherlyn glanced at Muloka, who quickly turned his face away from her.

'Respect!' shouted a very tall Aetherian standing by the Master's white chair. He frowned and gave Sherlyn a terrible glare.

Mooney held Sherlyn's hand. 'We have expected to sacrifice ourselves in the first place,' he said. 'That's why we're here, right? We can't go back now.'

'Um, technically,' The Master continued, 'all beings on planet Earth are unable to travel between the Partitions in free will, including us Aetherians. However, there is one special group of living things that has the ability to do so, and yes, it is the insects. The insects can go to whichever Partition without passing through Leap Holes, and that means that they can do so anytime, anywhere. Because of this, we use insects as media when we have to gather information about the other two Worlds. We attach our thoughts to the insects and use them as scouts. Do you remember the red butterfly? It was one of our scouts in Valeor.'

But Mooney shuddered. 'Does Ündia have the power to attach thoughts to insects, too?' He asked.

'We are not sure about that,' said the Master. 'But I'm certain that they have other ways to spy on the other Worlds. According to my knowledge, the Ündians can invade people's minds; but I have no idea how they do it.'

'I think that the Ündians were behind the attack of the black locusts before Rainbow Bridge,' said Mooney. 'If that is true, does Ündia know that we've come to Aetheria?'

'Possibly,' said the Master. 'But hopefully not.'

'It looks like your power is really limited.' Sherlyn said, frowning.

59

'We know more about Valeor than Ündia does,' said the Master.

'But who we have to fight is Ündia!' said Sherlyn.

'Aetheria is only a bit more developed than Valeor,' said the Master. 'We are not omniscient, nor are we omnipotent like how you might assume. This time, an alliance is to be formed between Aetheria and Valeor, and we have to depend on each other.' The Master lifted up his head and sighed. 'You can take them away now, Muloka,' He said, standing up. 'If you have any more questions, youngsters, you can ask Muloka.'

After the Master had left, Muloka held Colin by his hand and led the group out of the hall. 'Muloka,' said Sherlyn, 'you said Aetherians don't have desires and don't fight for anything, but I saw that the Master was quite proud.'

'Before we were born, we were already assigned to different tasks that we have to fulfill after we have grown up,' answered Muloka. 'This process of designation was done by pure chance. In this way, we don't have to fight for power; it's only the people in Valeor who would spend their whole life struggling for a desired position in society. In fact, every person is an important unit of the whole planet. In the universal point of view, every planet is the same and everybody is equal.'

Colin scratched his head, shook his shoulders and looked at Mooney. 'I don't care about whatever,' he said. 'It's all grownups' fault.'

* * *

As they walked together, Muloka saw that Jing was heavy in his steps. 'What's the matter, Jing?' asked Muloka.

'There're many things I don't understand,' said Jing, 'and I don't know where to begin. Well, I guess I will start with this: how does the lama from Tibet know about our mission? And how did he manage to find me?'

Muloka took a deep sigh. 'In fact, that lama was an Aetherian,' he said. 'He was an important politician in Aetheria before he was gone. We mourned for the loss of him. The Master has told you that normal beings cannot travel to the other Worlds freely, but I have also told you that in some cases, people do fall into Leap Holes accidentally and go to another World, the chance for them to return being very little since they might not be fitting into a Leap Hole again. And for us Aetherians, returning from a Leap Hole accident is impossible – at least nobody has ever come back in our history. Also, an Aetherian body decays soon after it reaches Valeor, and so the Aetherians must attach their spirit to a Valeoran body in order to maintain life. Jing, that lama fell into a Leap Hole about a thousand years ago, and every time when his Valeoran body dies, he has to find another body – mostly that of children – to attach himself to it.'

'Then how do you communicate with him?' asked Sherlyn. 'I mean, you obviously exchanged information.'

'Yes,' admitted Muloka. 'Remember we can attach thoughts to insects? Valeorans, even special ones, cannot communicate with the insects that carry our thoughts. Only Aetherians can.'

'Then, why doesn't that lama attach himself to insects and go back to Aetheria?' said Sherlyn.

'You have to understand,' said Muloka, 'that his Aetherian body is already lost, and what's left behind is his spirit. There is no point for him to exist as an insect in Aetheria Moreover, once an Aetherian has lost their body, they also loses their ability to attach thoughts to anything, including insects – he can only receive messages from us.'

'That is terrible,' said Colin. 'How long does he have to stay that way?'

'Until his spirit dies,' said Muloka.

Then Mooney lowered his head and said, 'Do you know, then, what would happen to the Aetherians who dropped to Ündia?'

'Hm…let me think,' said Muloka. 'I don't remember anyone going to Ündia. Some of our people went to Valeor and never came back, but some was gone missing for a while and then returned. Those people never said where they've been, and we never bothered to ask, since they might have just gone lost in the wild outside of the cities.'

'So,' said Mooney, 'is there any Ündians in Valeor and… Aetheria?'

Muloka shook his head. 'I don't know,' he said. 'We're not even sure if they can travel through Leap Holes.'

Suddenly Colin flattened his month. 'Muloka,' said Colin, 'do objects in Aetheria drop into Leap Holes, too?'

Muloka smiled. 'We invent a lot of things, and many of them have gone missing. Don't worry – the cloth is yours once you've found it.' And Colin smiled again.

'But I still don't understand,' said Jing: 'why didn't that lama from Tibet tell me all about the mission? Why did you have to use the Black Sphere to do the job for him?'

'When he was still in Aetheria, the plan for the mission has not been made. And we can't attach too much on the insects, you know,' said Muloka.

'When I was inside the Black Sphere,' said Mooney, 'I thought, how did anyone call for the Emissary for the first time? And can you not do the same this time, without using the Stonehenge?'

'We need the Sacred Jewel to call for Him,' said Muloka. 'That stone came to Earth along with the Immigrants, falling to the Partition of Aetheria by pure chance. When we used it, we had to muster energy in order to activate it, and the energy we gathered last time has already been used up. The cost for that energy was great: we Aetherians can no

The Mission of Mooney Rooney

longer stay under the sun like we once did, and we have to hide ourselves in caves. So the Emissary is afraid that if we used the Sacred Jewel again in Aetheria, our Partition would be destroyed.'

'Then what would happen if you use it in Valeor?' said Mooney. 'Is Valeor going to be destroyed?'

'The Emissary said that the force hidden within the land-marking of the Stonehenge in Valeor is enough to activate the Sacred Jewel, and that extra energy will not be required,' said Muloka. 'But if you ask me how the Stonehenge works, I can tell you nothing – it's beyond the intelligence of you and me.'

'Where is the Sacred Jewel?' asked Colin.

'It's in our keeping,' said Muloka.

'Who is the Emissary?' said Colin.

'I'm not sure,' said Muloka. 'I only know that he is in charge of the whole planet Earth. If you have a chance, you can ask the Highest of Aetheria about it. But the Highest seldom sees ordinary people.'

There was silence for a while. But then Jing got bored of the walk and said to Muloka, 'Why do you still have to walk while you have such high technology?'

'What's bad about walking?' said Muloka. 'Technology isn't always beneficial – it carries side effects, more or less. Most of us walk inside the cities; but if we are in a hurry, we'll use flying clouds. Outside, we'll always fly, because we cannot stay under the sun for too long. Nonetheless, time is nothing to us – we live long lives for about six to seven hundred years, some even over a thousand. And I am about two hundred years old now.'

'So when the people of our World come to "heaven,"' said Colin, 'they think that you all have eternal lives!'

Muloka held Colin's hand, looked at him and smiled. 'The Valeorans always thought that they would have eternal life once they come here. But now that you know, what they understand is indeed quite little.'

Chapter 10
The Training

The training camp was located at the northeast corner of the city. The camp was constructed with large cubic blocks, which were covered by a hemisphere that looked like a giant eggshell. There was a big crevice on top of the hemisphere; the entire building was surrounded by a wall of about fifteen feet tall, and there didn't seem to be an entrance anywhere.

Muloka walked to the wall, and told the four youngsters to walk in single file and put their hands on the shoulders of each person in front. Following Muloka, they went right through the wall. 'You have to do this by yourselves next time,' said Muloka.

They have come into one of the blocks inside the building, and they saw furnishing which resembled that in their homes. 'For your convenience, we are trying to do our best to make you feel at home.' He flipped his arm up, and at once there appeared a monkey that was exactly as tall as Colin. Muloka then pressed on the monkey's head, and the creature started to move immediately. 'I have implanted a chip inside this monkey,' said Muloka. 'His name is Kaga, and he understands most of what you say. He is here to take care of you. Oh, one more thing: including you, six of the seven groups of youngsters have arrived. Before the last group comes, I can take you to tour around Aetheria.' The youngsters leapt up in joy. 'I'll see you tomorrow!'

The next morning, the four youngsters got up for breakfast and waited for Muloka, who had come early. 'We can look around this city first, and then we will go outside to the forests,' said Muloka. 'Today you can choose to ride any animal you want – what animal would you like, Colin?'

'I want a horse!' said Colin.

So Muloka make a circle in the air with his arms and recreated a flying white horse for Colin, who immediately got onto the animal's back with help from Mooney. In the same manner, Sherlyn chose a black flying leopard, Jing a flying tiger, and Mooney a flying elephant. The wings of these animals were all wide and feathered, and Sherlyn swore that she had seen a picture of her leopard on the internet before. This time, instead of standing, Muloka sat on his flying cloud and flew by the side of the youngsters, leading them up and down over the city.

'There are more than five hundred cities in Aetheria,' said Muloka, 'and they are all built inside mountains. The total population in our World is about twenty million, and so each city holds about five hundred thousand people in average. Due to the fact that each city is gigantic and that such large mountains are hard to find, we have to travel very far until we meet another city. This city is named Dectolda, the smallest of all cities in Aetheria. Yet, it is the core of political affairs.'

'Well, if each city is so big,' said Sherlyn, 'then why do you call them "cities," not "countries"?'

'I don't know,' said Muloka. 'Maybe it's because we don't have racial differences in our World. Although each city can operate on its own, all of Aetheria is under the govern of the Highest.'

Jing looked down from his tiger and saw some Aetherians building small settlements. 'What do you do besides working?' He asked Muloka. 'Do they have entertainment at all?'

'What's entertainment?' said Muloka. 'Oh! Is that the thing you use to kill boredom in Valeor? Well, work is good enough for us. In addition, the Highest has wiped out all of our desires centuries ago, and now, I guess, our work is our already entertainment.'

Jing widened his eyes. 'That sounds…pretty dull,' he said.

'If one doesn't even have desire in the first place, how is one going feel dull at all?' said Muloka. 'Aetherians don't have a slight concept of what entertainment is. Oh, I remember something about you, Jing! You grew up in a temple, right? Haven't the monks there taught you how to put away your desires? I see that you still haven't learned – what kind of pupil are you?'

Mooney, Sherlyn and Colin all laughed at Jing, who lowered his head and blushed. 'I can't control what I want sometimes,' he said.

'It is precisely because human desires still exist in Valeor,' said Muloka, 'that makes it easy for Ündia to invade your minds.'

'We need to have desires in order to move forward,' said Mooney. 'It is our competitiveness that improves our World and makes it a better place.'

'No, no,' said Muloka. 'What is improvement? When is the end of it? The Valeorans have been developing for so long, but look! History can teach them nothing – they have been repeating what they have done wrong, and it seems to me that now they are having even more problems than before. So, is this improvement: using machine guns instead of you fists? In our World, as I have told you, we are assigned to different tasks before we are born, and we have no desire to become a person more than we can be. Everyday, we live only for our assigned tasks, since we know that all of us are important units of the World, and that if one single unit falters, Aetheria is not Aetheria.' The four youngsters scratched their heads and didn't quite understand. 'Ha, never mind,' said Muloka. 'You'll get it when you grow older.'

The five of them now flew low above the streets, where people waved their hands and smiled at them. 'We are a bit different from you,' said Muloka: 'we have no families. Our everyday work is all scheduled by unit leaders, and there's no conflict between people since we are only responsible for our own business. Moreover, we don't work within a time limit – we work until we have finished our task of the day.'

'That's yucky!' said Sherlyn. 'You guys are no fun – like robots.'

'Perhaps,' said Muloka. 'But what's bad about that? The people in your World desire to go to "heaven," but do they know what "heaven" is like? If it's like Aetheria, where everybody exists like a "robot" throughout their "eternal life," is "heaven" still desirable?'

Sherlyn hesitated. 'Well,' she said slowly, 'there are written records about what "heaven" is like in the Bible, but –'

'I believe that "heaven" is not really Aetheria,' said Muloka, 'and that "hell" is not Ündia, as you might have perceived. Well, probably it's all misunderstandings of the Valeorans!'

Mooney had noticed that Muloka did not have any facial expressions as he talked. 'Do you have emotions or feel happy and sad?' He asked. 'I see you smile sometimes, but most of the Aetherian faces are very grim.'

'We do have feelings,' said Muloka, 'but we don't go as deep as happiness and sadness. We feel physical pain, too, but we won't let it trouble us by generating emotions. Actually, the continual development of science and technology in Valeor has paralyzed the Valeoran's emotions – aren't Valeorans turning themselves into "robots," too?'

'Hey!' said Colin, giving Muloka a glare. 'Could you leave Valeor alone? And, you talk too much.'

'Okay, my fault,' said Muloka, who let out a smile and quickly hid it away.

So they were silenced for a long while. They continued to fly above the city, watching strange people and buildings below them. Suddenly Mooney realized something and sighed. 'Some people in our World want to go to a better place like "paradise," but in fact, they don't understand that there's no such place.'

'We're always like that,' said Colin. 'All of us desire for the better and are never satisfied with what we have. Just like now: we're in "paradise" and still not satisfied.'

'Hey! You talk too much,' Muloka smiled as he said softly to Colin. 'What's so bad about Aetheria?'

'They don't have meat here,' said Jing. 'Not even chicken.'

'Aren't you a vegetarian, monk?' said Sherlyn. This made the youngsters laugh; and Muloka, seemingly to have lost control, laughed too, and a strange feeling started to build up inside his heart.

'Hey, why can't I see any plants in the city then?' asked Jing.

'You're a good observant,' said Muloka. 'We leave the plants outside of the city in order to let them grow better. Let's go outside now – from there!' He pointed his arm to the left and flew out of the mountain.

The youngsters had already been outside when they first arrived; but today, after a night of sleep, they were eager to take a closer look at the beautiful environment again. They rode freely on their beasts, now through valleys, now over meadows. When they came to a lake, the beasts flew low on its surface and splashed water onto the faces of the kids, whose laughter echoed among the beautiful mountains of Aetheria. The strange feeling tickled inside Muloka again, drawing out the sweetest smile on his face that had never been known before…

On the back of their beasts, Jing raced Mooney across the forest. He yelled and cheered like Tarzan, but Mooney was steady on his elephant

68

The Mission of Mooney Rooney

and finished before him. 'This is so fun,' said Jing, flying slowly back to Muloka. 'Why did Aetheria destroy all the animals?'

'We didn't destroy them,' said Muloka. 'We only put them into another state of existence.'

'Why did you even do that?' asked Jing.

'It was because they were too aggressive in killing,' said Muloka.

'But haven't you broken the food chain and destroyed the ecosystem by doing that?' said Mooney.

'The gaps in the food chain are filled in automatically by new species of living things,' said Muloka. 'That is how nature works. Look at those yellow flowers on the plains and the trees on the mountains: they have well adapted to a world with no animals. There's nothing on Earth that is fully dependent on another thing.' Sherlyn, resting on her leopard besides Muloka, wanted to argue with him, but she opened her month and said nothing.

'But you didn't make the insects disappear,' asked Mooney, fondling with a small cluster of Wandering Mist.

'The insects are a strange group of animals,' said Muloka. 'We are unable to disassemble them.'

'Oh, of course, but that's not important,' said Jing. 'Is there fish in the waters?'

'So there will be sushi for you to eat, right?' Sherlyn teased him.

Muloka smiled. 'There're only plants underwater too.'

'You guys really talk too much,' said Colin. 'I've had enough. Let's go and play!' At once his white horse dived into the forest and strode like a bewitched arrow among the trees. For hours, the four youngsters found themselves in the forest chasing after one another, forgetting all about the perils that they were to face in the near future.

'Hey!' yelled Muloka. 'It's time to go back!'

69

But Mooney flew to him and said, 'Can we go to another city and look?'

'There's no time today,' said Muloka. 'Perhaps we will, someday.'

So the five of them flew back to Dectolda.

* * *

Inside an enormous, high-roofed indoor arena, the twenty-eight youngsters from Valeor were sitting in assigned seats in groups of four. They were all below the age of fifteen and were wearing Aetherian clothes, which were specially coloured in red, orange, yellow, green, turquoise, blue, and purple respectively for the seven groups. Their seats forming a large circle altogether, they sat silently with eyes surveying one another, knowing that they were all chosen to be special.

Then a group of Aetherians, led by a female Aetherian, showed up on the stage before the youngsters. The escort seated on the stage, with the female in the middle and seven other followers, including Muloka, by her sides. This female was rather thin, and she looked grim without a smile. 'I believe that you have already met the Master of this mission,' she said to the youngsters, 'and should be very clear of what you are here for.

'This is the training camp, and it has been used by Aetheria to train warriors. You all know that you carry special abilities, and now, you are here to get trained in order to become stronger. I'm the Monitor, and you ought to listen to my commands.' She glanced through the faces of each youngster, and continued, 'Okay. Now I give you the first test – get ready.'

She flung her left arm in the air. At once, a golden trail of light flashed out of her sleeve and spun around in the arena twisting in spirals. The head of the trail was moving so fast that none of the youngsters could see what it was until it came to a stop at the centre of their circle – it was an animal, resembling a golden rat, having a pair of long feathered wings grown on its back. 'Competing against the other groups, you have to catch this rat. You can use any methods,' said the Monitor. 'There is a prize for the winner group – you can start now.'

With wings quivering and eyes stirring, the golden rat sat on the ground and waited for the challenge. A smart-looking Hispanic boy stood up first and took action for his group, group yellow. As he sprang from his seat, his arms elongated to more than ten feet to reach for the rat, which immediately slipped away from his hand like a piece of soap. 'Perfect!' cried another boy from group green as the rat flew toward him. He opened up his arms, and at once faint lightning shot out of his palms and directed straight to the rat. Instantly, the rat was held still in the air and disappeared in front of everyone. But the youngsters could still hear the flapping of the wings – the animal had only become invisible, and was now even harder to catch. At this moment, Mooney held out his hands and looked at his partners, who too reached out their hands together and locked themselves in a circle. As they closed their eyes, their minds became one, listening to the sound of the wings flapping. Suddenly Mooney cried, 'Go!' and at once Sherlyn threw Jing several yards up into the air. Taking out his stick from his back, Jing gave out an echoing cry, and bang! The golden rat was revealed lying still on the floor. A loud applause was given to group red.

'Very well,' said the Monitor. 'Teamwork is the best weapon. Remember to use it to overcome hardships during your mission.' The Hispanic boy from group yellow gave Mooney a quick, unfriendly stare and looked away.

'These seven people beside me are your group guides,' continued the Monitor, 'and I think you've already got to know them. Now, please follow them.' And she turned and walked away.

'Wait!' said Sherlyn. 'What about our prize?'

The Monitor looked at her in the corner of her eyes. As she moved her left arm, a small stone floated slowly through the air and onto the palms of Sherlyn. This stone was no bigger than a ping-pong ball, and was blue like a glittering sapphire. 'Use it well!' said the Monitor, who turned and left the arena. The seven groups of youngsters then followed their guides to exit at the front. 'What is this thing, Muloka?' asked Sherlyn. And Muloka said, 'It is a wish stone. May it be a help to you when you are in need.'

* * *

Inside a dark chamber, the four youngsters of group red each stood with their backs against the four walls of the room. Muloka, standing at the centre of the chamber, held something tight in his hands that gave out radiance between his fingers. 'Face out your palms towards me,' he said, tossing the thing in his hands up to the ceiling. The light from the object shone on the palms of the youngsters, who felt a stream of pain piercing through their hands. So they withdrew their hands quickly and looked at them, and they saw that there were cravings that glowed faintly on their palms. 'Don't be afraid,' said Muloka. 'This is a form of direct energy, and it is used to upgrade the power inside you. The markings on your palms will disappear once your body has absorbed the energy completely, and the method to achieve that is left for you to figure out.' And he left the chamber.

'To figure out a way to absorb this energy?' said Sherlyn. 'How do we do that?'

Jing thought for a bit. 'Let's try sitting in meditation like I used to in the Shaolin Temple,' he said. Then he sat on the ground, folded his legs, put his hands on his knees and closed his eyes. The others had no choice but to follow him.

'Are you all ready?' asked Jing.

72

The Mission of Mooney Rooney

'Yes,' said the others.

Jing took a deep breath. 'Okay. Now,' he said slowly, 'focus to nothing but your inner self. Search for your thoughts and listen to them. Then, throw all of them away into the abyss and think of nothing...'

'It's hard to think of nothing,' said Sherlyn. 'Our brains are always working, and it's hard to focus on nothing.'

'Okay,' said Jing. 'Let's do it this way then. Count in your hearts: one, two, one, two...until you totally forget about your existence.'

So they tried. Not knowing how much time had gone by, Jing opened his eyes and saw that the cravings in his palms were gone. However he also saw that the three friends of his were lying deep asleep on the floor.

'Hey!' yelled Jing, scaring the three of them, who jumped up and apologized. 'Oh, actually,' said Jing, scratching his head, 'I'm the one to be sorry. I've been doing this for years, but this is your first time after all. Well, you see, my markings are gone already, meaning that this method does work. We can try doing this in a much simpler way – reading a sutra.'

'A sutra?' said Sherlyn. 'I'm Christian – I don't read sutras!'

'I am Christian too, but who cares about what sutras,' said Mooney. 'We are not going to understand what the content means anyway.'

So they read out the Heart Sutra after Jing, until they have memorized all of the verses. For two days, Jing sat on the floor and watched the three of them walking around the chamber and murmuring the sutra – it seemed even to Jing that they had gone crazy. 'Look!' cried Sherlyn suddenly. 'The cravings are gone!' And as if Muloka had been watching them all along, he came into the chamber and said, 'Well, that was quick. Now, your powers have been upgraded – let's go outside and try them out.'

Coming to an open space, Sherlyn made an attempt to jump under the bidding of Muloka. To her surprise, she launched herself to more than ninety feet up in the air, faltering a bit due to the shock. As she fell, she touched the ground with her toe and leapt up again. She was now breathing deeper than ever, feeling astonishing. With flawless movements, she landed on the ground without a stumble.

It was Jing's turn. He assembled his stick and performed the Ba Gua trick: currents of wind twirled like typhoon around the Ba Gua Shield, which expanded as Jing continued to stretch his shoulders. Following the trick, he jumped up in the air, raised the stick and smacked it on the ground – a deep, long crack had split the ground into two. Jing's robe still wavered under the shadow of the Ba Gua Shield, and he looked fiercer than ever.

Muloka laughed. 'Now, let's see what Colin and Mooney can do,' he said. 'Colin, your mental connection with Reddash should be much stronger now – you might even use it as a weapon. And Mooney–'

Suddenly, Muloka's hair quivered vigorously. Looking nervous, he glanced at the four youngsters in front of him and frowned. 'Come with me,' he said.

The five of them rushed to the entrance hall of the strange rock castle, and saw the Master, the Monitor, and the seven other groups of youngsters arriving with their guides. 'We have detected a moving object in the area of the Translucent Chamber,' said the Master, 'and the object has attempted to break in to the Chamber. This kind of things has never happened to us before, and we suspect it to be a conspiracy plotted by Ündia. I'm sorry for putting my suspicion on you, young Seedlings of the Emissary, and we apologize.'

'Why would you suspect us?' said Sherlyn. 'We have come here to sacrifice ourselves for the sake of the planet, and if you think that we are spies, you could send us back home and we can live our own lives happily and not care about Aetheria and what Translucent Chamber.'

'I understand how you feel,' said the Master. 'Although this is an alliance between Aetheria and Valeor, we still have to be careful of everything. As you said, it's for the sake of the whole planet.' He sighed. 'Now,' he continued, 'I'm afraid that Ündia has already begun their first step by attaching thoughts to other beings.'

'So do you suspect that we are Ündians?' said Sherlyn.

'We've invented a new device to detect the presence of Ündians,' said the Master. 'And now, please pardon us to use the device on you.'

'What if it doesn't work?' said Sherlyn. 'What if it like, breaks?'

The Master paid no attention to her anymore. At his signal, a guard opened a black metal box, revealing a glass-like sheet attached to its center. This sheet was as big as a person's face, and was made out of thousands of moving white particles. The box that was attached to the sheet appeared to be some kind of machine of high technology. The guard walked first to a girl from group purple and put the sheet in front of her face. The white particles moved rapidly, and after a while, the sheet turned into a mirror and revealed the girl's face. This happened to all youngsters that were being scanned, save when the test came to the Hispanic boy, the small particles moved for a long while before revealing his face, and the guard gave him a glare and walked away. Finally, the scan was over, and the Master said, 'We're very lucky to have discovered no Ündian conspiracy among you. But remember: the Translucent Chamber is a very important place, and you shall not go there.' Then he got up and left.

After going back to the training camp, Mooney asked Muloka, 'What happened, actually?'

'The Master is really worried upon detecting a spy breaking in to the Chamber,' said Muloka. 'As you might probably know, that place is extremely crucial to us – and therefore, Sherlyn, please don't misunderstand the Master, since his concern is necessary.'

'What does that box do actually?' asked Sherlyn.

'That is an Ündian detecting device,' said Muloka. 'We're afraid that the Ündians would invade our minds like they do to the Valeorans in Valeor, so we invented that mirror in order to reveal the true form of a being. The mirror has never failed us. Though, we haven't found a hidden Ündian with our mirror yet.'

But Mooney was too curious about the incident. 'Where's the Translucent Chamber, Muloka?' He asked. 'What if we went in there by accident?'

'The Translucent Chamber is designed by the Master himself, and it is hidden somewhere in that Rock Castle of his,' said Muloka. 'It contains the information of how to locate the Sacred Jewel.'

'How to locate the Sacred Jewel?' said Mooney. 'Didn't you say that the Jewel is in Aetherian keeping?'

Muloka lowered his head and was silenced.

'So, is the Jewel lost?' asked Colin in a low voice.

'In fact, we don't even know where the Jewel is,' said Muloka.

Chapter 11
The Translucent Chamber

Carrying a thick, old book in his hands, Muloka showed up in the training room early in the morning today. He put the book on the table and said, 'Kids, this book here is old – I found it in the library for you. It is so ancient that it was written in Aetherian, which we no longer use nowadays. But there are a lot of instructions recorded in there, of how you can practice your skills.

'Ündia is a dangerous place, and what we know is limited. This book doesn't teach you how to attack your enemies, but to defend yourselves against them using skills, like, surviving in extremely cold and hot environments, becoming invisible...'

'Becoming invisible!' cried Jing happily. 'Let's learn that first. But can we make our clothes to become invisible, too?'

'No, unfortunately,' said Muloka. 'You could only learn how to become like a chameleon.'

'That's good enough,' said Mooney, 'as long as we remember to take off our clothes after becoming invisible.'

Jing giggled. 'And if someone mixes up the order–'

'You're so stupid, you know?' said Sherlyn.

And they opened the book and looked at it together.

'Aren't these the same kind of characters written on Reddash?' exclaimed Colin.

'Yes,' said Muloka. 'You're a genius to have understood Aetherian by yourself.'

But Mooney scratched his head. 'They look like Hebrew characters to me,' he said.

'They are very similar to Hebrew, but absolutely not Hebrew,' said Colin. 'I know some Hebrew.'

'Anyhow,' said Muloka, 'let me interpret these records for you.'

For five days, the four youngsters stayed at the training camp and practiced according to the instructions written in the book. Sometimes Colin went outside and used his new tricks on Reddash: now he could just stand on the ground and wave his hands at the cloth, manipulating it without sitting on it. After learning how to change the colour and shape of the cloth, the little boy stayed at Muloka's side all the time, begging him to teach him how to recreate animals. The guide then taught him some basic skills on gathering the Mists, and after a while, the boy was able to make some strange small animals which bounced and tickled Mooney, who had been very quiet for the past few days.

Today, the four youngsters were practicing on the grounds as usual, when the Hispanic boy from group yellow came to them. 'You've done well in front of the Monitor last time,' said the boy with a Spanish accent, 'and now I wonder how powerful you've become in these few days. You want to see who's better?' He stretched and twisted his body before Mooney, who stared at him and didn't speak. But Jing stepped forward and touch his nose with his own. 'You want to fight, you stupid little twister?' he said.

'Go back to your practice,' said Sherlyn. 'What do you think you're doing? Haven't you had enough with the mirror last time?'

The Mission of Mooney Rooney

The boy stepped back. 'What mirror? I...just want to see how good you guys are.' And at once he stretched his arms to Jing trying to grab him by his neck and waist. But Jing flipped back in two summersaults, took out his stick and aimed for the boy's head. But the boy elongated his arms which, like snakes, clutched on to the stick and went straight for Jing's shoulders. 'Stop it!' cried a person from behind – it was Muloka.

'Caro, I do not want to see you starting fights here in Aetheria,' said Muloka. 'Go back to where you were!' And the boy turned and left. 'Don't think too much about the mirror, Sherlyn,' said Muloka. 'He's just a kid, like you. Mooney, how're you doing?'

'Not that great, Muloka,' said Mooney. 'The music in my head is in chaos, and I can't think clearly.' He then paused a bit, and continued, 'Something's been bothering me – some sort of vague signals inside my head. They're like warnings, but...I don't know, Muloka, I can't think.'

'Let me try sensing your brain waves,' said Muloka, whose hair quivered for a while and then stopped. 'That's strange – I can't sense anything either. Well, just take it easy, perhaps. It'll get better.'

In the midst of sleep the following night, Mooney felt pain in his left small finger and woke up. He saw that there was a black cockroach standing right next to his left hand. Excluding its antennae, this cockroach was about five inches long, and Mooney had no way to communicate with it. Then, the cockroach flew out of the window; seeing that the others were asleep, Mooney climbed out of the window and followed it.

The streetlights had become dimmer at night, and Mooney ran closely after the low-flying cockroach. After some time, the cockroach came to the Master's Rock Castle and flew vertically up to the very top of the building. Mooney stood on the ground, took a deep breath and floated up in the air – he had already learned how to float in the past few days of training. Like a balloon, he went up to the roof of the castle and landed there. The platform was no smaller than two acre, being the largest rock of the building. First, Mooney could see nothing; but gradually, as the cockroach started to spin around on the ground, there appeared a tall Aetherian man standing twenty yards away from Mooney. The cockroach then flew to the shoulder of the man and rested there. The man didn't speak, but he pointed up his finger to the dark roof of the city: now Mooney noticed a huge rock of irregular shape hanging in the air behind the castle. The floating rock was about twenty yards wide and was rotating slowly on its own.

'Here,' said the tall man, 'is where the Translucent Chamber is hidden. I want to make a deal with you.'

'Who are you?' asked Mooney.

'You don't have to know who I am,' said the man. 'You only have to go in to the Chamber, come out, and tell me its secret.'

'You are Ündian!' shouted Mooney.

'You're a smart boy,' said the man.

'Why don't you go in there yourself?' said Mooney.

'I tried,' said the man. 'But there's a special protection shield around this rock, and I couldn't go in. Later, I found out that if one uses his mental power to minimize the energy his own body gives out, then he will be able go through the shield without being detected. I've spotted a boy named Caro to do the job for me, but I found that his brainpower is not enough. You are here to fill in for him.'

'What?' challenged Mooney. 'Do you think I'd ever help you?

'Respect!' shouted the man. Immediately Mooney recognized this man – he was the very tall Aetherian who shouted at Sherlyn when the group met the Master for the first time. But he kept the surprise to himself.

The Mission of Mooney Rooney

'You're too innocent,' said the man. 'Ignorant, like the Aetherians. You think you can win over us? There's no way, kid. The Highest of Ündia has already known all about your plans; but he won't stop you being stupid, because he knows that Ündia will always win. You see, Valeor is already under our control: the Valeorans are cursing and killing each other just the way we want. And Aetheria has taken no effort on improving itself – silly, silly, silly. You know how powerful Ündia has become? We're probably even stronger than that so-called "Emissary" now! Join us: with your exceptional mental power, you can become our ambassador in Valeor.'

'You're not good enough to conquer Valeor!' shouted Mooney.

'Wow, wow. Valeor's failure is all because of the Valeorans themselves, my friend,' said the man. 'It's because they couldn't throw away their desires, making us easy to feed them, invade them.'

'Not everybody in Valeor is a failure,' said Mooney.

'True,' said the man, 'but those unusual ones will die off soon. History could teach you nothing – do you remember the prophets and mystics who once lived in Valeor? They told the Valeorans to cast away their desires, loves, hates, and their own selves – but have you ever listened? Well, it's lucky for Ündia that you haven't. Very soon, we are going to be King of the Earth – it would be wise if you join us, Mooney.'

Mooney thought for a while. 'We can talk about that later, can't we?' he said to the man. 'Now tell me how to get into the Chamber.'

The man laughed. 'Well,' he said, pointing to the floating rock behind him, 'the shield around this rock is invisible, and it detects any form of living energy near it. If you minimize the energy your body gives out, you'll have no problem going through the shield and enter that rock. You'll find the Chamber then.'

'Why do you want me to go there anyway?' said Mooney.

'Because that's the only way to find the Sacred Jewel,' said the man.

'Why? Does Ündia want the Jewel?' said Mooney. 'Aren't you more powerful than the Emissary already?'

'Are you going or not?' said the man.

'Sure, but I might betray you,' said Mooney.

The man laughed again. 'Look at your small finger!'

Mooney saw his small finger and was shocked: there was a fine black trail that traced from the cockroach bite to the centre of his palm. 'This is the gift my cockroach has given you,' said the man. 'If my cockroach lives, you're fine; but if it dies, for whatever reason, the poison will circulate your whole body, which is not going to be fun. This time, instead of you controlling it, this insect is going to control you!'

Mooney shuddered. But he thought that it didn't matter if he died, but that if this man in front of him lived any longer, Aetheria will be in danger. 'Very well,' he said. 'What do I do after I enter the Chamber?'

'The Chamber was designed by the Master under the command of the Highest of Aetheria,' said the man. 'No one has been there before. So you will be the only one to figure out what to do inside.'

So Mooney closed his eyes and concentrated. The warmth of his entire body now moved slowly into his inner chest, down to his abdomen, and was gone. 'Okay. Now, where should I go?' asked Mooney.

'Get yourself under that big rock, if you will,' said the man.

Slowly, Mooney walked towards the floating rock. When he gets near to the area underneath the rock, he stopped, for he felt something blocking his way. He tried to touch it with his hands, and found that it was an invisible staircase. So he climbed carefully up the stairs and reached the bottom of the rock, which received him by opening up a small hole. He got in.

He saw nothing inside the rock – it was nothing but a cave. He searched the ground and the wall carefully and still found nothing.

But he remembered the name "Translucent Chamber" – the Chamber must be invisible, he thought. So he closed his eyes and tried to sense the location of the Chamber by pure feeling. Very strangely, he felt that his spirit left his body and wandered around inside the rock; when he opened his eyes again, he saw that he was enclosed by four luminous but translucent walls, and that himself had also become invisible. He saw that at the centre of the Chamber there was an invisible sphere glowing, and he walked to it...

'Hello there – are you from Valeor?'

Mooney fell to the ground in horror. He turned around, and saw a glowing but translucent man sitting on the floor behind him. With hair floating loosely, this person looked like an Aetherian. 'Why have you come here?' said the man. 'Do you know that this is a forbidden place?'

Mooney was astonished. This person's voice was so kind that it seemed to echo forever in his heart.

'I came in by accident,' said Mooney.

'No, no, my child,' said the man. 'Nothing on Earth is by accident. Everything is set from the very beginning. Well, since you have come, I shall tell you something about myself. I have been sitting here thinking for hundreds of years, but I still haven't reached a conclusion. Perhaps you could help me.'

'Thinking for hundreds of years?' said Mooney. 'I'm...not too good at thinking, and I don't think I could help you.'

The man sighed. 'Sometimes my mind turns in circles and gets nowhere,' said the man, 'not even back to the beginning.' He stood up and walked to Mooney. 'Come! Let us see.'

Mooney had never saw eyes as bright as this man's. He was tall, and his face shone kindly on Mooney's own. Through the glowing light, he showed no signs of aging on his face, though he must be old. As he smiled and took Mooney's hand, Mooney felt a stream of warmth creeping slowing toward his chest from the man's palm, and the feeling was more comfortable than ever before. 'This sphere here,' said the man, 'has troubled me for hundreds of years. Do you want to take a look at it?' Mooney nodded, and put his hands on the sphere. He felt that there were tiny little bumps on the surface of the sphere, which seemed to be creating a pattern of some kind. Some of the bumps were higher, some were lower, some thicker, and some thinner; all the bumps were clustered together, forming a spiral that twisted counter-clockwise from the top and to the bottom of the sphere. Mooney blew some air to the spiral, and said, 'Can you turn it?'

'No,' said the man. 'I've tried many times.'

'Try again,' said Mooney.

The man tried turning the sphere with his hands, but it didn't move at all.

'Can you try moving it some other way?' said Mooney.

The man glanced at Mooney and didn't speak. He then put his right hand horizontally above the sphere and closed his eyes: the sphere stirred and started to rotate, gradually increasing in speed.

'Faster, faster!' cried Mooney. So the man put his hand above the sphere again, until its speed had become so great that Mooney could no longer see it spinning. Now Mooney heard something whispering inside the Chamber. It was a melody.

He closed his eyes and listened. 'Okay,' he said after a while. 'You could stop the sphere now.'

'You're doing great,' said the man.

Mooney fell into deep thought. Then he began to sing. 'This song is in G major,' he said. 'But the melody line doesn't seem to be complete.' He walked around in the room and sang for some time. He improvised another melody to fill the missing parts of the song, and abruptly a change occurred to the sphere...

84

There appeared two glowing sentences on the surface of the sphere. 'It's Aetherics,' said the man.

'What do they say?' asked Mooney.

The man laughed. 'I'll translate them for you:

Over Valeor the highest cloud cries
In tears of Aether, the Sacred Jewel lies

'You see?' he said. 'Everything is planned from the beginning, and our meeting today is not by accident. The problem is now solved, and you can go.' And the man couldn't stop laughing in great joy.

'Should I keep secret of what I've seen?' said Mooney.

The man nodded. 'And,' he said, 'I've cured the poison that you carried in your palm. I don't know why and how you got it, but right now, all is well.'

Mooney looked at his own hand and saw that the black line was gone. 'Who are you?' asked Mooney.

'Who I am is not important,' said the man. 'Farewell; and we shall meet again.'

'How do I leave?' asked Mooney.

'In the same manner as you came in,' said the man.

So Mooney sat on the floor and closed his eyes again. As he found that the walls around him were gone, he also saw that his body had turned back to normal again. He walked down the staircase from the cave and saw the Ündian-Aetherian man waiting for him.

'What took you so long?' asked the man nervously. 'Did you find anything?'

'Well,' said Mooney, 'I did find something. But I still have to think about it before I tell you.'

'Tell me now!' shouted the man furiously.

'I've already found out your secret,' said Mooney. 'If I told you, would I still live?'

'You…!'

'Don't worry,' said Mooney. 'I still carry your poison and I can't escape from you. Let me think about it first! Oh, is it morning already? I've got to go now!' Like a feather, Mooney dropped himself to the ground floor from the roof of the castle and ran straight back to the training camp. To his own surprise, he ran at least five times faster than he could before – was it because of the stream of warmth given to him by the man inside the Chamber? Mooney wondered.

Chapter 12
The Plan

Sherlyn woke up and saw that Mooney was gone. She was worried and called in Kaga the monkey, asking him where Mooney had gone. Kaga shook his head.

'Where's Mooney?' said Jing, getting up from bed. 'We have a meeting this morning, and we can't be late.'

'Don't worry about him,' said Colin. 'He can take care of himself.'

Today was the sixth day of their training, and the Monitor was holding a meeting in the arena. Sherlyn, Jing, and Colin arrived there the latest, and Muloka saw that Mooney's seat was empty. 'Why are you late?' asked the Monitor. 'And where is Rooney?'

'Here!' The door opened, and it was Mooney. Sherlyn, Jing, and Colin ran to him and brought him to his seat. 'Where were you?' whispered Sherlyn. 'Did you get into trouble or something?'

'There's no trouble here in Aetheria,' said the Monitor.

But Mooney looked at her. 'Do you really think so, Monitor?' he asked.

'What do you mean?' said the Monitor.

'Well, what if you found an Ündian in Aetheria – that would be real trouble, eh?' said Mooney.

Abruptly the Monitor stood up from her seat. 'You mean you've found an Ündian?' she said coldly.

'No, no,' said Mooney. 'I said "what if." Please, don't be too nervous.'

The Monitor sat down. 'We're still not sure of what we might do if we found an Ündian.'

'Oh,' said Mooney. 'So that means if I was Ündian, you wouldn't know what to do?'

'Mooney!' said Muloka.

'What's wrong with you?' whispered Sherlyn. 'Did you find something?'

'I'll tell you later,' said Mooney, who then stood up and said loudly. 'If you're still not sure of what you would do, you should start planning – now.'

'It's true, Monitor,' said a boy from group blue. 'If you don't have tactics against Ündians, then what are we here for?'

'Danger and death!' cried a girl from group turquoise.

'Aetheria has been in peace for a very long time,' said the Monitor, 'and we don't have much experience on strategy making. But Mooney, why do you behave like this today – do you know something?'

'I got up this morning and saw an Aetherian from my window,' said Mooney. 'That man looked strange, and so I went out of the window and followed him. But then after a while, I lost track of him, and so I suspected that he was a spy.'

'Oh, I see,' said the Monitor. Suddenly her hair shook, and Muloka looked nervous. Noticing this, Sherlyn clutched Mooney's arm. 'Be careful,' she said; and Jing had got his hand ready on his stick.

Carrying four white metal net-like objects, six armed guards came in from the side doors and stood in front of the Monitor. Those objects were about seven feet long, and they were shaped like bananas. 'Get him!' cried the Monitor.

So the guards put three of the four objects together to form a cage, while two of the Monitor's watchmen ran to Mooney and picked him up. But Jing took out his stick and swung it at the heads of the watchmen, who, to Jing's surprise, retracted by bending their bodies back almost ninety degrees. 'Jing! Don't be rude!' cried Muloka.

Sherlyn stood up. 'Monitor!'

'We have no choice,' said the Monitor.

'What do you mean?' said Sherlyn. 'Don't you dare to treat a Valeoran like this! There are twenty-eight of us here, and do you want to put us all into cages?' At once all the other youngsters stood up and stared at the Monitor.

'Don't forget, girl,' said the Monitor, 'that here is Aetheria, and you're only Valeorans.'

'You better take that back,' said Sherlyn. 'We're here to sacrifice ourselves – we are the ones who're going to fight Ündia, while you Aetherians will be sitting here and watch. Don't you dare to put Mooney into that cage!'

'It's okay, Sherlyn,' said Mooney, who shook off the hands of the guards and walked into the cage himself. 'The Monitor has her reason. Actually, this cage looks interesting. You know I always like to try new things.' And he closed the door of the cage.

'Mooney! No!' cried Sherlyn, who ran to the cage and shook it as if she had gone mad. 'Want do you want from him?' she cried at the Monitor.

'We don't accept people who lie,' said the Monitor. 'And this boy has lied to me. This cage is designed to capture Ündians, and if he still doesn't speak the truth, I'll send him to the Master. Today I was going to teach you how to enter Ündia, but I think we have to postpone that now.'

'Mooney, do you have anything to tell me?' said Sherlyn.

Mooney shook his head.

'If he does, he would've told the Monitor about it,' said Colin.

'Well then,' said the Monitor. 'Take him to the Master.'

Mooney was then taken to the hall of the Master and was surrounded by hundreds of administrative Aetherians and the all the other youngsters from Valeor. By the side of the Master, there stood the traitor who looked at Mooney as if nothing had happened the night before.

'Mooney,' said the Master in a low voice, 'I don't believe that you're our enemy. But the Monitor is reasonable in her suspicion. Do you have anything to say?'

'What could I say?' said Mooney. 'You don't trust liars, do you?'

'That's why we've put you into that cage,' said the Master.

'That's not fair,' cried Sherlyn. 'You can't just put him in there because he lied. Get out that mirror and see if he's really Ündian.'

'Yes, Master, we should do that,' said Muloka.

'There's no need,' said the Master. 'We've done that once already, and I trust you, Mooney. Well, let's do this: if a youngster could break open this cage, then Mooney shall be free.'

'That's not fair either...' said Sherlyn. But Mooney told her to stop talking.

Jing was first to step up to the challenge. He felt the cage with his hands and realized that it was actually not metal, but some kind of soft substance. He then hammered the cage with his stick, but the cage yielded a little bit and had no signs of breaking. Then Caro went up to the cage and put his arm into one of the holes of the net. He then filled his arm up with all the flesh he had, until his whole body was absorbed into the arm, bulging like a huge, fleshy potato which widened the hole of the net. However, as he retracted his body, the enlarged hole sprang back to its normal state.

A girl from group purple came up. 'Sorry Mooney,' she said. 'But please be patient.' Then, as she put her hands on the net-like cage, blue flames crept along the surface of the cage and set it on fire. 'Stop it! Stop it!' cried Mooney. And then a boy from group orange came up and shot out laser beams from his fingers, trying to cut open the cage. Still, the cage stood there, unscratched.

The twenty-seven youngsters stood there and discussed amongst themselves. But Mooney sat down and whispered some melodies in the corner of his lips and, after a while, a line of crimson entered the hall through the edge of the door, crept along the walls and onto the cage. Sherlyn took a closer look at the visitor and found that it was nothing but a troop of ants! Getting larger in number, the ants climbed onto the cage and started working – there were so many of them that Mooney could hardly be seen anymore. Gradually, the cage was bitten open, and Mooney emerged from the insects, which then left under Mooney's bidding.

'Wow!' said Colin. 'What are those things?'

'They're called fire ants,' said Mooney. 'I called them in from just outside of this city. I didn't know they are that good though!'

'So now,' said Sherlyn turning to the Master, 'we have to decide whether or not we are going to stay here anymore. If you don't even trust us, how can we be allies?'

'Aetherians only value on what is right and what is wrong,' said the Master. 'We did nothing wrong by suspecting Mooney. Even now, before he tells the truth, we still have to beware of him.'

'Oh,' said Sherlyn. 'Okay then. Let us go home now, Mooney.'

'If you really want to,' said the Master.

But Mooney shook off Sherlyn's arm. 'It's enough,' he said. He then turned to the Master and said, 'I've decided to work with you in the first place. If you suspect me now, I have nothing to say. But you will figure out the truth very soon.'

'Okay,' said the Master. 'Now go back to the camp.'

In their room, Sherlyn nervously asked Mooney about what happened, but Mooney told her not to speak just yet. He took out a black felt pen from his backpack and drew a line from his small finger to the centre of his palm. He then closed all the doors and windows of the room, and said, 'This is a very serious matter. Listen carefully...' He then told them everything, save the old man and the sphere he saw in the Chamber.

'What I did in the Master's hall was only for the traitor to see,' said Mooney.

'But what are we going to do?' asked Sherlyn. 'Should we tell Muloka?'

'No,' said Mooney. 'Just wait, and you'll see.'

The four youngsters had not seen Muloka for a few days and were practicing on their own. But they could feel somehow that someone was watching them. Today, Muloka showed up while they were practicing on the grounds. 'I've been talking with the Master,' he said, 'but he still wants to observe you for a longer period of time. He also forbids me from seeing you.'

'But has he found anything?' said Mooney.

'No,' said Muloka. 'And I want to tell you that I trust you. But I know that wouldn't help.'

'Oh, yes that would,' said Mooney.

'How?' said Muloka.

'Please tell the Master not to spy on me,' said Mooney. 'I will explain the whole thing to you later, but for now, trusting me is the most important thing.'

'If you don't tell me, I can't do anything for you, Mooney,' said Muloka.

92

The Mission of Mooney Rooney

But Colin went to him. 'Please, Muloka,' he said. 'You are the only person we can count on now.'

Muloka sighed. 'Okay,' he said. 'I will do my best for you.'

* * *

Three days after the surveillance on Mooney was cancelled, Mooney went again to the top of the Master's castle at midnight and saw the traitor as he had expected.

'I've been waiting here for you for three nights!' he said furiously.

'Well, I'm here now,' said Mooney.

The man laughed. 'Though they've cancelled the surveillance, they'll still capture you first if anything bad happens to them,' he said. 'But if you join me right now, the Aetherians will not be able to hurt you.'

But Mooney frowned and said, 'I've been seriously thinking about joining you. But how am I going to tell my friends? I've already lied to them about it, and I don't want to do that again. How could I allow myself to betray them?'

The man laughed. 'You silly Valeoran,' he said. 'I really can't understand the way you think. Well, I mean, you can tell them to come join me as well. For now, I want you to tell me everything you saw in the Translucent Chamber.'

'That is rather difficult,' said Mooney. 'I saw some words, but I don't know what they say or mean.'

'What words?'

'I told you I couldn't read them.'

'Well, well...just tell me, and let me...'

'Okay,' said Mooney. 'I am going to write it out for you.' He then pointed his finger in the air and wrote several glowing characters by leaking out some internal energy. 'Ah...wait, let me think...hm...I can't remember. Let me think again...' And the glowing characters faded away.

93

'Don't play with me, kid!' said the man.

'I really don't know that language,' said Mooney. 'Plus, I still carry your poison. Don't worry: I will talk to your Master about it immediately after I join you. Now, give me some time to think.'

'I'm the Ündian Master in Aetheria,' said the man.

'Oh!' exclaimed Mooney. 'You're the Master here? Do you mean there are other Ündians here?'

'Of course,' said the man. 'But you don't have to know who they are.'

'But how do I recognize them?' said Mooney. 'Very soon I will be Ündian too, you know.'

'You will know sooner or later then,' said the man. 'We have our own way to recognize each other.'

'Like what way?'

The man paused. 'Stop talking – write!' he shouted.

'I really can't remember the whole thing,' said Mooney. 'What if you bring me to your Ündian hiding, if you have any? Perhaps I'd think more clearly there.'

The man hesitated. This kid doesn't seem to be lying, he thought, and it is true that he couldn't cause much harm, but…

'You better do so before I lose my memories,' said Mooney.

'Okay,' said the man. 'I will get some men to take you to my hiding tomorrow. Are you bringing your friends too?'

'No,' said Mooney. 'But I'll bring them next time. Why don't you come and get me yourself?'

'I'm one of the servants of the Master of Aetheria, and if I left him, it will be too obvious.'

'Then how am I going to know if the people I see tomorrow are Ündian?' asked Mooney.

'I told you we have our own way to figure it out,' said the man.

The Mission of Mooney Rooney

'What way?' said Mooney.

Then the man glanced at Mooney's left hand and said, 'We have many Ündians in Aetheria,' he said, 'and we've hidden a mark somewhere in our body.'

'Where?' asked Mooney. 'I can't see you carrying any special markings.'

'Think, kid,' said the man. 'What part of your body is not used here in Aetheria?'

'Oh – is it your…' Mooney pointed at his own lips, which were stiff like stone.

The man opened his month, and revealed a thing sitting on top of his tongue. It was a small black snake which flipped its own hideous tongue and hissed at Mooney. Mooney was so shocked that he fell to the floor.

'You don't have to be scared like this,' said the man. 'You're not Ündian; not yet.'

Chapter 13
The Ündian Hiding

Before dawn, Mooney got back to his room in the training camp and told his group mates about his conversation with the Ündian.

'Good job, Mooney,' said Jing. 'You're going in to their hiding and take them out!'

'Well, I can't do that alone,' said Mooney. 'This time I go there, hopefully I'll return with some useful information.'

'I understand what you mean,' said Sherlyn, 'but I still think it's too dangerous. Do you want me to tell Muloka?'

'I do trust Muloka,' said Mooney, 'but after all, we don't know which Aetherians are Ündian.'

'Then let me go with you to the hiding,' said Sherlyn.

'No,' said Mooney. 'I don't want anything bad happen to you. Don't worry – I'll be fine.'

During training today, Mooney went alone to the washroom and met an Aetherian man in the hallway. Revealing the black snake in his month, the man took Mooney by his one arm and made a flying cloud big enough for two people with the other. Then, in five seconds, the two of them flew out of Dectolda.

The Mission of Mooney Rooney

'Where're we going?' asked Mooney. But the man didn't seem to hear him at all. Since there weren't any landmarks outside of the mountain, Mooney tried to remember the direction, speed, and duration of their flight as much as he could.

As the sun started to sink into the west, Mooney and the man came to a lake which was surrounded by a great valley. Mooney was stunned by the beautiful green colour of the lake and the mountains that appeared as though they were painted in crayon – Mooney remembered: this was Lake Louise! Mooney went to Lake Louise in Alberta with his parents when he graduated from elementary school; but how strange it was for him to see the lake here in Aetheria! Now the hair of the man quivered, and slowly a rectangular hole opened up at the surface of the lake. The two of them then dived into the hole...

*   *   *

The other three youngsters saw that Mooney was gone and were worried. They then went to find Muloka and told him everything.

'Oh dear!' cried Muloka, walking around nervously. 'How am I going to explain to the Master? Oh no...let's...let's go see the Master now.' Although Sherlyn knew that they couldn't speak of the matter in front of the Master and his servants since the traitor was among them, she kept that to herself and didn't tell Muloka.

In the hall of the Master, Muloka told everything to the Master who then toddled around his chair and spoke nothing. Sherlyn noticed several servants by his side, but couldn't recognize which one was the traitor.

Finally the Master said, 'This is too sudden. Before we find out where Mooney is, the three of you have to be isolated.'

'That I think is unnecessary,' said Muloka.

'It doesn't matter, Muloka' said Sherlyn.

So the three of them were put in a room inside the castle of the Master, and Muloka visited them frequently. 'Don't be too worried, Muloka,' said Sherlyn. 'Mooney has his own plan.'

'Do you know what he's going to do?' asked Muloka.

'It's not time for me to tell you just now,' said Sherlyn. 'Just believe in Mooney!'

*   *   *

Slowing down, Mooney and the man descended along a narrow tunnel and into a huge, hollow, cylindrical track. Standing on the cloud, Mooney looked around him and saw that there were many levels of space along the wall the cylinder, and that there were people working on different tasks on each level, where strange looking machines and facilities were built. Their cloud stopped somewhere around the middle section of the cylindrical track and flew slowly into one of the levels on the wall. The man then handed Mooney over to another man before he left; the other man looked Aetherian, too, but had a pale golden belt around his waist. That man put Mooney in a room, gone for a few minutes and came back. 'Sorry to have kept you waiting,' he said, smiling. 'I went to put a language chip (we stole it from Dectolda) inside me in order to talk to you. Nice to meet you: my name is Ralph (you can call me Ralphy), and I'm, eh, the manager here. Please, if I don't speak well enough, pardon me. I haven't seen a Valeoran before.'

But Mooney couldn't speak a word. This person was too polite to be an Ündian; or had Mooney's perception on Ündians been wrong?

Ralphy had a round face and a pair of big eyes, and he smiled at Mooney all the time. 'What's this place?' Mooney asked him.

'Ho, ho,' laughed Ralphy. 'This is an Ündian base. All Ündians in Aetheria come here. We're one big family here sticking together in this foreign place, and we…'

The Mission of Mooney Rooney

'Base?' said Mooney. 'What kind of a base?'

'Oh,' said Ralphy. 'A base for the destruction of this place. You know, the place up there. Hm…I'll tell you about that later, since I can't do so without Roxter's permission. Oh yeah, Roxter told you to write down things about the Sacred Jewel, is that right? But how the heck would you know anything about the Jewel, ah?'

Mooney wanted to laugh so badly. 'Well,' he said, 'I don't think I have to tell you that – I'm sorry, but I mean no offence. Now I need to find a place nice and quiet, sit there to refresh my memory.'

'That's not a problem,' said Ralphy. 'You can walk around here, until you've found a place you like.'

'Really?' said Mooney. 'Thanks. Can I have pen and paper then?'

'What pa?' said Ralphy. 'Do you mean you need something to write with? Gosh, we don't have any here. You can't do your task without them?'

'Do you have anything to help me express my thoughts then?' said Mooney.

Ralphy thought for a moment, and suddenly there appeared a luminous stick like a conductor's baton in his hand. 'Use this to draw on the walls if you like,' said Ralphy.

'Thanks,' said Mooney, who then wrote two glowing Aetherics letters on the wall. 'That's all I can remember for now,' he said. 'I guess I need some rest after the long journey today.'

'Take your time, take your time,' said Ralphy.

'So can I walk around this level now?' asked Mooney.

'Sure,' said Ralphy, 'as long as you will finish your task. Just follow me, if you want to go sightseeing.'

'Ralphy,' said Mooney, 'why do we have to know about the Sacred Jewel anyway?'

'I have no clue, my friend,' said Ralphy. 'I only listen to orders; I don't even know what the heck the Jewel is.'

So the two of them walked together on that level of the Ündian base. Having a high ceiling, the level contained some very neat, shelf-like structures that held thousands of small cubicles, each covered by lids.

'What are these shelves?' asked Mooney.

'These are hives,' said Ralphy; 'but they're not for bees.'

'What are they for then?' said Mooney.

Ralphy opened one of the lids and revealed the animal inside. It was a big black cockroach, and Mooney was certain that it belong to the same species as the one that bit him. 'It's asleep right now,' said Ralphy, 'and it won't hurt you. We have over ten million of these little fellows here.'

'What do you keep them for?' asked Mooney.

'For killing Aetherians, of course,' said Ralphy.

'How?' said Mooney.

'Hm…I'll tell you later,' said Ralphy. 'You better go back to your room and take some rest for now.'

The next day, after Mooney had written down two more letters, Ralphy brought him to another level for sightseeing. There, Mooney saw some similar shelves that contained cockroach eggs and younger cockroaches. There were some workers feeding them.

'These workers look Aetherian,' said Mooney. 'Are they our prisoners?'

'No,' said Ralphy. 'They're all our own fellas.'

'That means that they all keep a little snake in their mouths?' said Mooney.

'Oh Roxter's told you that eh? Yes, they all do,' said Ralphy. 'You want one now?'

'No, no,' said Mooney immediately. 'Not now – may be later. So, do these workers work here all day? How come the Aetherian government doesn't notice that they are missing?'

'Their government doesn't pay much attention to such little things,' said Ralphy, 'since all Aetherians think that they are having peace, and are not aware of danger.'

'I see,' said Mooney. 'So what are we planning to do to the Aetherians?'

'I don't know,' said Ralphy. 'Roxter hasn't told us what to do yet, other than to feed the cockroaches.'

'Ah, then, how do you remain contact with Ündia?' asked Mooney.

'Hm…well, you don't have to know that yet. You better go back to your task now, since I think that Roxter will come for you tomorrow.'

So Mooney went back to his room and completely wrote out the first of the two lines.

The next day, the traitor came – he was Roxter. He went to Mooney's room, saw the sentence on the wall and was in thought. 'Do you understand what that means?' asked Roxter.

'Of course not,' said Mooney. 'I don't even know what that language is.'

'I can imply from what you've got here that there is another sentence following it,' said Roxter.

'You understand what it says?' asked Mooney. 'Can you explain it to me?'

'Shut up and write out the other sentence!' Roxter shouted, scaring Ralphy to almost squeezing himself to death at the corner of the room.

'But that's all I can remember,' said Mooney.

'You have to remember it all!' howled Roxter. 'You know I will kill you if you don't listen to me.'

'There's no use killing me,' said Mooney calmly. 'Ah, what if you let me go back to the Translucent Chamber to look at it one more time?'

'That's a good idea, Master,' said Ralphy in a trembling voice.

Roxter gave Ralphy a fierce glare and turned away to face the glowing sentence on the wall. 'Fine, kid,' he said. 'Now come with me.' And he brought Mooney away.

It was midnight as they came again to the roof of the Rock Castle. 'Wait here for me,' said Mooney, and he walked toward the invisible staircase.

'Of course,' said Roxter coldly. 'If you don't come down, you know what's going to happen.' He revealed his cockroach sitting on his shoulder.

Mooney smiled and climbed up the stairs, then came back down after a while. 'Have you seen it again?' asked Roxter nervously. 'Write it out now!'

'Let's go back to the base first, and then I'll write it out for you,' said Mooney.

'Now!' said Roxter. 'You're going to forget it by then!'

Mooney sighed. He took out the glowing stick and wrote something on the floor of the roof; he scrambled the words around, making it "In the Sacred, lies Aether Jewel of tears."

'What?' said Roxter puzzled. 'What does that mean?'

'How would I know?' said Mooney. 'That's what I saw.'

These words really are Aetherics, thought Roxter, and this kid can't be playing tricks on things he doesn't understand. 'Good,' he said. 'Your task is finished. Well, I wanted you to join us in the first place, but now, since you've caused such a delay, I don't think you'd fit to become an Ündian.' He then grabbed his cockroach from his shoulder and said, 'You'll be dead in three minutes, my friend.' And as he crushed the insect into a stinky black paste, Mooney fell to the ground, appearing to be in immense pain. 'You…you broke your promise!' he said.

Suddenly, in the midst of Roxter's laughter, there appeared a wall of white robes above the Castle. As Mooney had expected, it was a muster of Aetherian warriors, led by the Master and Muloka.

Roxter flung his left arm into the air and shot out a shaft of light that pushed the Aetherians back a little. Then he hopped on to his flying cloud and headed for exit; he looked at Mooney in the corner of his eyes and saw that he was still lying in pain on the ground. As Roxter tried to escape, the Aetherian guards threw out four banana-shaped objects which speeded themselves directly to Roxter. But the traitor waved his hands in the air and surrounded himself with a thick mist which blinded the Aetherians temporarily. After the mist was gone, the banana objects were found on the roof of the Castle, having formed a cage but caught nothing. Now the guards lifted up their heads and saw that Roxter had already gone miles away. So they took to their flying clouds and chased after him.

Muloka and the Master ran to Mooney and helped him get up. Like dead, Mooney fell to Muloka's lap, and Muloka held him tight in his arms. Suddenly Mooney whispered, 'Don't speak. Let the traitor go.' At once Muloka understood. After quivering his hair beside the Master, he took Mooney back to the training camp.

The coming of the Aetherian aid to the Castle wasn't an accident – it was Mooney who had planned it all. He remembered the protection shield that surrounded the rock above the Castle, and that the shield was used to detect any form of living energy near it. When Mooney walked through the shield, he didn't minimize the energy that his body gave out, knowing that in this way, the Master would get noticed and come up for the Chamber.

'Muloka,' said Mooney, 'please pretend that I'm dead and let Roxter go. And, except for the Master, don't tell anyone what I told you.'

'What about your friends?' said Muloka.

'Where are they?' asked Mooney.

'They're still in the Master's Castle,' said Muloka. 'I will bring them to see you whenever I can. Now stay here in your room, and I must go see the Master.'

Chapter 14
The Encounter

Mooney was sitting alone with the Master inside a small room, when Muloka opened the door and let in Sherlyn, Jing, and Colin, who rushed to Mooney immediately in tears of delight. Muloka stood and watched them as they hugged, and saw something so lovely and beautiful that he had never seen before.

'We have let Roxter go,' said the Master. 'Thank you very much for your help, Mooney. So, now, can you tell me your whole story?'

Then Mooney made up a story that excluded what he saw and did inside the Translucent Chamber.

'I'm sorry for suspecting you, Mooney,' said the Master.

'There's no need for you to be sorry, Master,' said Mooney. 'There are still many Ündian spies around us, and you have to be careful not to tell anyone that I'm alive. You must tell all of Aetheria that I'm dead, in order to loosen Roxter's defense.'

'Do you remember where the Ündian hiding is?' asked the Master.

'I remember its direction and distance from Dectolda,' said Mooney. 'And I also remember that the place is very similar to Lake Louise in Valeor.'

'That's perfect,' said Muloka. 'The Three Worlds on Earth share the exact shaping of land. And Aetheria and Valeor have very similar geological features on some locations.'

'Should we capture all the Ündians in Dectolda first before we take any actions?' said Sherlyn.

'I'm afraid we would alert the whole Ündian population in Aetheria by doing so,' said Mooney. 'How are we going to capture them all anyway?'

'I have an idea,' said Sherlyn.

These few days, Mooney spent all his time in a room with the Master, discussing strategies on attacking the Ündian base. Sherlyn, Jing, and Colin were back in the training camp, pretending to mourn for the death of their friend, Mooney.

For health's sake, it was announced that all Aetherian administrators were required to take a regular body check-up starting today, and Muloka Jibrelle was in charge of the dental and oral section. First, he checked the six other group guides and found no snakes in their mouths. He then performed the check-up with the other administrators, including over twenty people who refused to open their mouths. Muloka and the other group guides then locked those people up in individual cages and forced them to open their mouths. Eventually, the guides found out that five of these administrators had bad teeth and were shy, and that the rest of the captives were all keeping snakes in their mouths.

Upon the result of the check-up, the Master sighed. 'What a shame for me to have kept this many Ündians by my side without knowing!' he said.

'It's not too late, Master,' said Muloka. 'Now what are we going to do with them?'

'They're Aetherians after all,' said the Master. 'It's only that their minds are invaded by Ündians. If we kill them, we'll kill the bodies as well as the primary minds of our own people. So before we find a way to force the Ündians out of their minds, we'll have to lock them up. Meanwhile, the next step is to destroy the Ündian base. But as I have told Mooney, I don't want to use violence, since it's not the Aetherian way.'

'But I'm afraid that we have to use violence against the Ündians,' said Mooney. 'To my knowledge, they'll use cockroaches as their weapon. And so, I think that we should find a way to kill those cockroaches first.'

'Mooney,' said Muloka, 'how come your poison's gone?'

Mooney widened his eyes and could utter no reason.

'Are you hiding anything from us?' asked Muloka.

'It's okay, Muloka,' said the Master. 'Now we should figure out a way that would work against the cockroaches.' Then the Master nodded at Mooney – at once there seemed to be an understanding between them. Mooney remembered: the Translucent Chamber was designed by the Master, so would it be...?

Together with a group of Aetherian warriors, the twenty-eight youngsters were gathered in the hall of the Master, along their group guides, the Monitor, and the Master. 'Today,' said the Master, 'we are going to figure out a way to take out the Ündian base with the least involvement of violence. First, I have to tell you how we are planning to capture the Ündians from their base.'

Holding a black metal hoop, Muloka stood up beside the Master. This hoop had a diameter of about a foot and was no more than two inches thick; it was constructed with tiny devices of high technology, and one could notice small glowing spots embedded in the material. 'This is our latest invention used to capture Aetherians whose minds are overtaken by Ündians,' said Muloka. 'This hoop is made of a special metal called the Freedom Alloy, which expends and shrinks according to the user's orders. Inside this hoop, there were numerous manipulating chips that can be used to take temporary control over an individual. Let me show you how it works.'

He tossed the hoop up in the air and waved his hands at it in a distance. Floating, the hoop expanded to about nine feet in diameter, wandered a while in the air giving out a buzzing sound, shrunk to less than four inches wide and then came slowly back to Muloka. 'This should be an easy job for you now, since you've been trained for more than two weeks in the camp,' said Muloka.

'So we're each going to carry one of these…hula-hoops for Ündians?' said one of the youngsters.

'Not just one,' said Muloka smiling, 'but many of them.'

'Now,' said the Master, 'we have got to figure out a way to kill the Ündian cockroaches. Any thoughts?'

'We can burn them,' said a boy from group green.

'We can't burn them all,' said the Master. 'There're too many of them.'

'How about using a net?' said a girl from group blue. The Master was in thought.

But Jing stood up. 'Um…' he said, 'I don't know if this works or not, but the Chinese people believe in something, some sort of rule that exists in nature. Well, we believe that all things in the universe are balanced. For example, all preys are predators and all predators are preys…'

The Master stood up. 'That is a very good idea,' he said.

The peaceful mountains and shores around the lake were now populated by Aetherian warriors and the twenty-eight youngsters from Valeor, who were all mounted on flying clouds and readied in their assigned positions.

Under the command of the Master, the Aetherian warriors inserted several massive rods into the lake. As the rods stayed in the water, the serene lake started to ripple and began to produce waves, which leapt high over the mountains. The pool was shaken open, and everyone waited, silently overlooking the roaring waves beneath the blazing sun.

Finally, the moment came. A hole opened at the centre of the lakebed, releasing a giant swarm of black mass which expanded rapidly toward the offenders. At the bidding of the Master, several Aetherians blew piercing notes out of some strange looking instruments, whose wailing blow echoed across the hills. At once millions of flying creatures came from behind the hills and invaded the sky above. These creatures resembled white cranes, except that they were much smaller in size and had longer beaks that were slightly flattened. Now the birds dived down toward the black mass and smashed their feathers and talons on their prey. The cries of the birds, the flapping of wings, and the clashing of the waves all joined together to form a symphony of conflict and dissonance...

The battle between the black and the white masses went on for minutes, until the hungry birds could see no more that they could eat. But as the birds took leave, a troop of Ündian-Aetherians rushed out of their base and shot out numerous black slender objects from their sleeves. These objects flew toward the white birds, killing several by twisting their necks – they were snakes, big winged snakes, which the Ündians bred in the deepest places of their World.

Now the white birds were all scared and were fleeing in chaos. Flying like a rain of arrows toward the shores and the mountains, the black snakes wrapped themselves around the bodies of the Aetherian warriors and sank their teeth into them. Helplessly, the warriors moaned and fell to their backs in tremendous pain. At the order of the Master, all warriors that were still standing got together quickly to form a great circle on the hillside. As they stretched out their arms, the Wandering Mists in the air gathered to form hundreds of eagles that flapped their wings immediately to meet the snakes, which all ceased to exist under the claws of the wild birds.

The Ündian-Aetherians turned and fled. Now the twenty-eight youngsters shot out their "hula-hoops for Ündians" from their arms and speeded them after the traitors. Buzzing like bees, each of the expanding hoops slipped around the bodies of the Ündian-Aetherians and was tightened around them. The traitors were brought high up into the air by the hoops, struggling for freedom that they would never be granted from the strong Alloy.

Suddenly, an explosion occurred to the Ündian base, forcing a giant pillar of water to shoot up vertically into the sky directly from the lake. 'It's Roxter!' cried Muloka. 'It seems that he has discovered the blueprint of the "Light Speed Capsule" – there's no way we can get him now.'

Water was splashed onto everyone. The catastrophe had ceased, and the lake had become half as deep as it used to be. Among the captives, Mooney spotted Ralphy. 'I'm sorry, Ralphy,' said Mooney.

'That's okay, my boy,' said Ralphy, smiling. 'You are just doing your job.'

So the encounter ended with cheers from the Aetherian side.

Chapter 15
The Highest of Aetheria

'Who is the Highest of Aetheria?' said one of the youngsters. 'What does he look like?'

'You're going to see him in a moment anyway,' said another youngster. 'We defeated the Ündians at the lake yesterday, and he's going to meet us. I wonder if he could grant me a wish or something. If so, then I'd have my whole family to move to Aetheria.'

'What's so good about this place?' said another. 'If you live here with your family, you'll be the weirdest person in Aetheria, since Aetherians don't have families.'

The youngsters laughed.

'So, the Highest of Aetheria,' said a boy. 'Isn't that God? Oh my God! How I long to see your face!'

'Man, he's not God,' said another youngster. 'Aetheria's not even heaven, so how come he's God? If he was God, then he shouldn't be called the Highest of Aetheria, but the Highest of Valeor, Ündia – the whole Earth!'

Under the lead of the Master and the group guides, the twenty-eight youngsters came before a snowy mountain peak where no trees grew. As they drew near to the mountain, two colourless staircases emerged from behind the peak, which then wrapped themselves around the mountaintop and joined to become a long corridor with pillars on its sides in front of the mountain. As the visitors entered the corridor, they could see rings of rainbows surrounding their path.

'This is amazing!' said Sherlyn.

'Yeah,' said Muloka. 'I have never seen the Highest either; you are so lucky to be seeing him at such a young age.'

'How should we call him then?' asked Jing. 'I mean, I am not going to finish every sentence with "Highest of Aetheria," that's kind of long and weird. Should I call him King or something?'

'That's not appropriate,' said the Master. 'Hm...how about calling him "Mr. President" as you would in Valeor?'

The visitors had now come inside a huge cave inside the mountain that was filled with gentle light. The Master looked up to a high place as his hair started to stir: slowly another wide colourless staircase stretched from the very top of the cave down to meet him. The visitors were standing in wonder as they saw a twinkling white halo suspended above the stairs behind a curtain of white mist. At that moment, Mooney heard a familiar melody hanging loosely in the air, and involuntarily he began to sing along with what he heard. Slowly, Mooney climbed up the staircase in front of him until he reached the top, where he could faintly see a figure emerging from behind the mist. The face of the figure was kind and peaceful, and his hair was white as snow. 'Ho! Here we meet again!'

'You...you?'

'Yes, it is me. I told you that we will meet again.'

'Highest of Aetheria?' exclaimed Mooney.

'Come and sit down by my side, son.'

'Do you live here alone, Mr...President?' said Mooney.

'Ha! "Mr. President"? Well, I do live here alone.'

The Mission of Mooney Rooney

'Oh,' said Mooney. He couldn't stop looking into the Highest's eyes. 'Do you feel lonely?'

'I don't feel it, because I have evolved to carry no deep emotions, just like other Aetherians. The reason why I asked you to come here this time is that I want to tell you about the Sacred Jewel.

'Since the Jewel could no longer stay in Aetheria after it was used for the first time, it was hidden long ago in Valeor by the Emissary, who has also put into that sphere we saw last time the clue to relocate the Jewel. For generations, the past leaders of Aetheria have failed to figure out the puzzle of that sphere, until last time I met you in the Chamber. Now, only you and I know about the secret of the Sacred Jewel; but I am old. You are the only one left to receive the task of finding the Jewel.'

'But I don't know what the riddle from that sphere mean,' said Mooney.

'You will, if you may think about it. But for now, the first thing you have to do is to find out the missing Hengestones with the other youngsters.' He took out a small golden envelope from his sleeve and gave it to Mooney. 'What's inside is the method to communicate with the Jewel. Keep it well.'

Mooney took the envelope from the Highest. 'How do I use it?' he asked.

The Highest smiled. 'You will know, my son,' he said. 'Let's go down now – the other youngsters are waiting.'

So the Highest walked side by side with Mooney. 'You told me that you've been staying in the Chamber for hundreds of years,' said Mooney, 'but now you say that you actually live here. I don't understand.'

'You might not understand this too well,' said the Highest, 'but what you saw in the Chamber was just my spirit.'

As Mooney and the Highest walked down the stairs together, the youngsters opened their mouths and were lost for words. Was this the very God that most of them had been praying to everyday? No, no, this was just the Highest of Aetheria, not the creator of the Universe. But their hearts kept insisting that this was the very spirit that they had been admiring and longing for, who had sometimes seemed so close to them, and sometimes so far away. And now, He was right in front of them.

The Highest of Aetheria walked down, carrying a smile of everlasting kindness and peacefulness. 'Ho, ho!' he said. 'Why do you look at me like this? Come!'

The youngsters laughed and surrounded him. 'Are you God, Mr. President?' asked a girl.

The Highest smiled. 'No,' he said. 'But does it really matter who I am?'

'I mean,' the girl continued, 'are…are you the God who's been living in our hearts all along?'

'If you really want to say so,' said the Highest.

'I guess there must have been a misunderstanding,' said Sherlyn.

'Well,' said the Highest, 'if you feel comfortable about the God that lives in your hearts, then never mind the misunderstanding.'

'You are so kind,' said a youngster, 'that you seem so much to be God. Can you do what God does?'

The Highest laughed. 'I'm like your God?' he said. 'What can God do?'

'He can do anything!' the youngsters cried.

'Do you really think so?' said the Highest. 'Children, there is a force that exists in the universe, and you can call it "God." This force is always there to keep the universe in order, but it might not be the "God" that lives as a father and friend in your lives. Try to think about this: what do you pray to God for? Why do you give thanks?'

The youngsters all burst out their answers at once. There was one boy who lifted his voice and said, 'I pray for a good night of sleep, and I

114

thank God for giving me nice clothes and food, because those are all the things I want. Why do you ask? Have I been doing anything wrong?'

The Highest smiled. 'You haven't. But the real question is—'

'The real question is why we want,' said a voice.

The Highest looked toward where the voice came from, and saw Colin standing by himself outside of the crowd. 'Come to me, child!' said the Highest. 'Come!'

Colin walked slowly to the Highest, who picked him up and smiled at him. 'What else do you have to say, son?'

Colin touched the nose of the Highest with his finger. 'And the other question,' said Colin, 'is why we always talk about me, me, and me.'

Then the Highest turned to the rest of the youngsters. 'Do you understand now?' he said. ' "God" is "God," and He is not subject to your wants and desires like you would expect Him to, because the idea of a self should mean nothing to Him, since He Himself is selfless from the beginning to forever.'

The youngsters scratched their heads and didn't understand.

'Ha!' said the Highest. 'May I talk less! Now, let us feast!' And immediately a colourless dining hall was revealed inside the cave, and the Highest led the youngsters to the big table at the center the hall, which was crowded with fruits and vegetables. The youngsters laughed and ate happily.

Suddenly a youngster said, 'Highest, who is the Emissary?'

'He is the being who moved the Immigrants to Earth,' he replied.

'Then why doesn't he stay here to look after us?' said one.

'I don't know,' said the Highest. 'Perhaps He's busy!'

And the dining hall was ever filled with laughter.

Chapter 16
Farewell

The training was finally over. Muloka had taught his four pupils the way to enter Ündia and told them about the approximate location of the Hengestone that they were responsible for. Also, for safety's sake, Muloka had put as many Aetherian inventions as he could into each of his pupils' backpacks.

Rather than smiling like he usually did, Muloka looked a little grave today. He had been feeling rather queer since the first day he met his pupils, and now the queer feeling was getting 'worse' as he would describe it. He felt that as if something had dwelled a hole in his heart, sucking all its fluids out, making it ever concentrated with its basic ingredients.

'What's the matter, Muloka?' said Mooney.

'I...I don't know,' said Muloka.

Colin stared him. And as Muloka looked back, his view blurred. 'What am I doing?' he asked himself. 'How come...?'

'The day of parting will come eventually,' said Colin; 'and now it has. Don't put too many thoughts into it, Muloka.'

Jing ran to them. 'What?' he said. 'Are we leaving?'

116

The Mission of Mooney Rooney

Muloka put his hands on Jing's shoulder. 'Are you going to miss me?' he said.

Jing looked strangely at Muloka. 'Why?' he said. 'Of course! But–"

'I've taught you everything you need to know,' said Muloka. 'And it's time for you to go.'

'Today?' asked Sherlyn.

Muloka nodded; and there was a while of silence.

The four youngsters then took off their Aetherian robes and changed back into their own clothes. Having well packed up, they were all ready to leave Aetheria. At the time they walked out of the training camp, Colin gave a big hug to Kaga the monkey. 'Thank you so much,' he said. 'What a nice pet you've been!'

Together on a large flying cloud, Muloka sat silently with his four pupils. The cloud was moving especially slow today; and as they glided among the Wandering Mists, Mooney sang in a low voice, which seemed to awaken the air of Aetheria from its slumber.

Since Valeorans could not go directly from Aetheria to Ündia, they must go back to Valeor first and then enter Ündia. Now Mooney, Sherlyn, Jing, and Colin had finally come before the Leap Hole from which they entered Aetheria, and Muloka said, 'Take care...' and tears rushed out of his eyes. It was, indeed, the first time that Muloka cried in his life. The youngsters, too, couldn't resist their emotions anymore. They threw themselves into Muloka's chest, bursting into tears.

'It's time to go,' said Muloka. Gently across the air, he pushed the four of them toward the Leap Hole...

*   *   *

Below the Rainbow Bridge, the four youngsters fell wearily onto Reddash. 'Let's go home,' said Sherlyn, and Reddash pointed its head straight to Vancouver.

'Wait!' said Mooney. 'We should go find Mr. Chubby first.'

'Why don't we go home first, and then go find him?' asked Sherlyn.

'We don't know what he has told our parents,' said Mooney, 'We've got to find that out before we go home.'

'But where is he now?' said Jing.

'Hm…we can probably find him in the hotel we stayed in last time,' said Sherlyn. 'Or at least we shall find some clues there.'

Reddash then turned back and landed under the hill behind the hotel. The four youngsters went straight for the receptions, but the manager of the hotel came to them at the door and said, 'Come with me – my guest is waiting.'

They knocked on the door of room 112. It opened slowly. 'What is it?' said a dreamy voice from behind the door. The four youngsters looked and saw a fat, bald man – who else could it be? 'Mr. Chubby!' they cried.

Dr. Ince looked at the children and couldn't believe what he saw. Since the youngsters left, he had been worrying about the safety of the kids, who were much too young to carry such a great responsibility. Yet, as he pitied them, he also admired them for being so selfless and ready to sacrifice themselves to the world for nothing. Now, the nameless heroes in his heart were standing right in front of him.

'Are these the children you're looking for, Dr. Ince?' asked the manager.

'Yes,' he said. 'Yes, yes! Oh come here, let me look at you!' He knelt down and saw Colin's face, which seemed to have gotten thinner than the last time he saw it.

'You look funny, Mr. Chubby,' said Colin. 'And you stink.'

'Oh, I'm sorry,' said Dr. Ince. 'I haven't bathed for three days already.' And the room was filled with laughter.

'I went home after you left,' said Dr. Ince. 'But later I thought that if I stay at home, you would never find me when you get back. So I remembered: when I was small, mommy said that if I got lost in a mall, I should stand at the same spot where I last saw her, and she'd come back there for me. So I returned to this hotel and waited for you; but when I still saw no signs of you after a month, I almost went crazy inside this room!'

'That's a joke,' teased Jing. 'Now I'm hungry!'

'Oh, food!' said Dr. Ince. 'But I should go take a shower first. Ah but food!'

The hotel manager smiled. 'You should go take a shower first, doctor,' he said. 'I'll bring the four of them to the buffet downstairs.'

'Gosh! The food in Valeor tastes way better!' said Jing, holding a chicken leg with his left hand and a lamb rib on his right.

'What?' asked Dr. Ince. 'What Valeor?' And Sherlyn explained everything to him.

'Wow,' said Dr. Ince. 'Wow. Who would have thought of that? So…do you have to go to hell, or…Ündia then? That's going to be more dangerous! I don't want you guys to go.'

Mooney smiled. 'Come on, Mr. Chubby! I've learned many things in Aetheria. You know, everything is planned from the beginning and we all work for our assigned tasks, purely for the sake of the whole planet. Therefore, we should not care too much about our personal benefits, but to look at the bigger picture of things. For example, say, if each one of us was a unit of a compound eye of an insect, we should listen to the orders of the insect's brain for where to look, instead of following our own likings. In this way, the whole eye could function as it was supposed to. If not, this eye was not an eye.'

'Wow Mooney,' said Jing. 'That's an awesome thought. But think less – try this lobster here, man! It's so good!'

'What are you guys planning to do next?' asked Dr. Ince. 'I want to do something for you, if I could.'

'We want to go home for the moment,' said Sherlyn. 'What did you tell our parents?'

'I told them,' said Dr. Ince, 'that you don't like your families and went away from home together. And later, you got kidnapped and are lost.'

A delicious ball of lobster fell out of Jing's mouth. 'How can you say that?' said Sherlyn.

Dr. Ince laughed. 'I'm just joking, kids,' he said. 'What I really told your parents is that you've joined a survival competition, in which you have to leave home and stay in the United States for a month. If you can survive alone in this period of time, without anyone providing anything for you, you'll bring home a hundred thousand dollar cheque.'

'Do they believe that?' said Sherlyn.

'I'm an important science figure in America after all,' said Dr. Ince, 'and it's not hard for me to ask the television channel to fake the whole thing out for me. And I've already given your parents some money, saying that it's the prize you get just for joining the competition. So I guess they are believing it.'

'What a thing you've done for us, doctor,' said Sherlyn.

'Oh, and Mr. Chubby,' said Mooney, 'I want to see the President of the United States – can you arrange that for me?'

'What?' said Jing hanging a string of spaghetti on the corner of his mouth. 'Are you kidding me?'

'Ah…that is…not quite easy, Mooney,' said Dr. Ince. 'He won't see you unless you have a good reason.'

The Mission of Mooney Rooney

'Alright,' said Mooney. 'Then we'll go to the White House right a way by ourselves.'

'That's gonna be fun!' said Jing. 'We can break in there while the President's asleep and scare him to a heart attack.'

Sherlyn hit his head and smiled. 'That's rude, Jing,' she said. 'Mooney, how should we break in to the White House anyway?'

'Oh, hold on!' said Dr. Ince. 'Don't do anything silly. Let me think about it…do you have a reason good enough for meeting the President?'

'We're telling him,' said Mooney, 'that we went to Aetheria, and that he as President must know about the danger that is coming to Valeor and the whole planet – isn't that a perfect reason already?'

Chapter 17
Greetings, Mr. Presidents

In a guest room inside the White House, the President of the United States smiled at the young visitors. 'Nice to meet you, young people,' he said. 'Dr. Ince told me something about you, which seems quite unbelievable. Although there are many things in the world that we cannot explain, but can you explain–'

'Yes, But will you believe us?' said Colin.

'You're almost ten years old – is that right, sir?' said Mr. President. 'You do have brilliant imagination. Come on – I'll let you see my face.'

'We see your face almost everyday on TV,' said Sherlyn. 'Don't you think you're more like a celebrity than a President who's supposed to be here to serve?'

'Well,' said Mr. President. 'I just want to be remembered by history, positively.'

'That's selfish,' said Sherlyn. 'The first thing you think about is yourself. You know what? It's this habit of yours that is making our World an easy place to be invaded.'

'Mr. President,' said Mooney, 'we're not here to tell you about our adventure, but to warn you about the danger that our World is going to face. I hope that the United States can lead the entire World to peace by telling all the people not to hate each other because of selfish reasons.'

'We've been keeping peace in the world,' said Mr. President.

Sherlyn turned to Mooney. 'He doesn't understand,' she said.

'I'm just saying, Mr. President,' said Mooney, 'that you should stop any warfare that has been going on in the World, since by doing so, there would be less killing in the World. Ending people's sufferings would also end their hate, and the World would be a much better place without hate.'

'Sometimes war is the only way to gain peace,' said Mr. President.

'What an excuse,' said Colin.

Dr. Ince was worried about the tension between the youngsters and the President. 'Uh...' he said. 'Mr...Mr. President?' But the President raised his hand and told him not to speak.

Suddenly the body of the President floated up into the air and lowered back to his chair again. But the President didn't show any signs of surprise, and said, 'There're many people in the World who carry special powers. But if you talk to me about what Aetheria and Ündia, it's just too hard for me to believe that. Okay, if I believed that, what could I do? Should I go on TV and say that the Ündians are everywhere and are coming to get us? What an idiot I would be!' He sighed. 'I believe that you're special, children, and I would very much like you to contribute your powers to our country. Think about it!' He then turned to Dr. Ince angrily and said, 'I don't have time for this kind of thing, Ince.' And he left.

Mooney was disappointed with his meeting with the President. 'Let's go home Mooney,' said Jing. 'We go do our own things and never mind that President guy.'

'I want to try again,' said Mooney.

'Actually, Mooney, you know we don't have to make him believe us right a way,' said Colin. 'Before he does, we can do whatever we like!'

Sherlyn smiled. 'That's an awesome idea Colin,' she said. She looked at Mooney and made a gesture with her fist. 'Oh!' cried Jing. 'That's gonna be fun!'

'You can't do that!' said Dr. Ince. 'You're going to break the law!'

'We don't care,' said Mooney. 'We've already risked our lives for our mission, and we fear nothing. But now, who I worry the most is you, Mr. Chubby. I don't know what the President will do to you.'

Dr. Ince gave out a weird giggle. 'Don't you worry, I shouldn't be always thinking about myself now. I should look at the bigger picture of things. I'm always on your side.'

Mooney was grateful. 'By the way,' he said, 'which countries do you think could influence the World the most?'

'What? What are you going to do?' said Dr. Ince.

'I'm trying to make my plan bigger,' said Mooney.

Hearing this, Jing got so excited that he jumped gently – gently though, his body launched out of the roof of the building and fell back to where he was. He then stuck his tongue out and apologized, when his friends had already laughed their eyes out.

'The main powers of the World are the United States, the United Kingdom, Japan, Germany, France, Russia, and China. The leaders of these countries get together regularly to discuss big things in the World, but they all think of benefiting their own nations only. They don't look at the big picture.'

'That's perfect,' said Mooney.

*   *   *

Dr. Ince gathered much information on the everyday lives of the seven big leaders of the World and gave it to Mooney, who then took out

The Mission of Mooney Rooney

his map, passed it to Colin who memorized all the directions of their destinations in a few seconds. Mooney also asked Dr. Ince to prepare some chambers somewhere – somewhere isolated – for his use.

They were all ready to go again!

It was two in the morning, when the four youngsters were hovering on Reddash above the White House and saw from the bedroom window that Mr. President was soundly asleep. Silently, Mooney used his mental power to carry him out of the window and put him onto Reddash. As Mr. President began to wake up, Jing poked somewhere behind his neck, and he fell back to sleep again.

It was overcast in London today, and Reddash was wandering above the British Parliament building. While the Prime Minister was having a conversation with the press, a thick mist surrounded him and took him away. Jing then pressed the spot behind his neck, making him fall asleep on Reddash.

After a meeting, the Presidents of Germany and France walked leisurely in a private park. Dismissing their bodyguards, the two of them went inside a newly constructed garden maze, where they never found a way out before ending up on Reddash.

Together with a large crowd of audience, the President of Russia was attending an outdoor presentation of a famous opera. In the midst of applause, the President disappeared at a flash of the red cloth, on which he was put to sleep, dreaming about the rest of the fantastic music performance.

Despite the heat, the Chinese President was visiting a public farm in the countryside of Beijing. Suddenly, a sandstorm became out of nowhere and blinded everyone in the farm. Nobody was hurt in the storm, but strangely enough, the President of China was gone.

At a golf course in Tokyo, the Prime Minister of Japan was getting ready to hit the ball with his new driver. At his powerful swing, everyone in his escort focused their sights on the ball that landed one foot away from the hole. As the escort cheered after the good hit, the Japanese Prime Minister was already asleep with the other leaders of the World up in the air.

Waking up, the World leaders each found themselves alone inside a small chamber that had a couch, some food, and a door that was locked. These seven chambers had no windows, and the leaders had no clue of where they were. The leaders stayed in their chambers for almost two days, and they were about to question their own sanity.

Suddenly the doors of the chambers opened, and the seven leaders ran out of their rooms at the same time. To their surprise, they noticed each other's presence in a larger, circular chamber, standing with their backs facing a single wall. At the centre of the chamber, there stood the four fearless youngsters, who stared silently at them. The leaders were overwhelmed with horror but didn't dare to reveal their emotions.

The President of the United States recognized the youngsters. 'This is too much!' he said. 'Do you know what is going to happen to a country when its leader is taken away? And now you've taken away seven of us! You know, even if you are children, you're breaking the law by doing this.'

'Nobody knew that we took you away,' said Sherlyn.

'I'm sorry,' said Mooney in a trembling voice. 'I know that we're being rude, but we have to no choice. Um…could you please show us your tongues?'

'We don't have time to play with you,' said the President of Russia. 'If you have anything to say, just say it.'

But the leaders felt something pulling their jaws down, forcing them to open their mouths. Fearing the power of the youngsters, the leaders had no choice but to stick their tongues out for them. 'Thanks,' said Mooney, smiling. 'You can put our tongues back into your mouths now.'

Then Mooney explained to the leaders about the danger that was about to come and the method to prevent it. 'I understand that you're good kids,' said the President of China. 'And I also understand that everyone wants peace...'

'You children are ridiculous!' said the President of Germany.

'I know you wouldn't believe us,' said Mooney; 'and we won't force you to. We just want to make a deal with you.'

'A deal?' said the Prime Minister of Japan. 'You know you're going to be punished for doing this.'

'We don't care about what punishment,' said Colin.

'We are here to ask you to stop the wars in the World,' said Mooney. 'We ask you to keep peace between the nations, and tell all the people in the World to throw away their desires, making them strong enough to defend Valeor.'

But President of France laughed. 'You think too ideal, children,' he said.

'Danger is drawing near,' said Sherlyn, 'and our World is not going to withstand it if you continue to stay like this.'

'If we agree to your deal, are you going to take us back?' asked the U.S. President.

Mooney smiled and looked at Jing, who immediately ran around to press the sleeping spots of the seven leaders in less than three seconds. As Colin took out Reddash and expanded it, Mooney used his mental power to lift the bodies of the leaders onto the cloth, which took flight out of the chamber as the ceiling opened...

Waking up again, the leaders sneezed and quivered. 'What's this place?' asked the Prime Minister of Japan.

'This is the top of the world – Mount Everest!' said Colin.

127

'Feeling cold?' asked Mooney.

'No!' said the seven leaders together.

The four youngsters had already learned the skill of enduring extreme temperatures, but the leaders were normal people after all, and should feel bitterly cold on the peak.

'We'll see how long you can stand,' said Mooney. 'Now please take your time to admire this wonderful place!'

'Why do you do this to us?' said the President of Russia.

Mooney didn't answer. But he saw that the world leaders were indeed old, and that they couldn't stand the cold anymore. So he told Jing to put them to sleep again, and brought them away from the mountain.

Waking up again, the leaders found themselves dripping with sweat. 'This is the hottest region of the Sahara,' said Mooney. 'Feeling hot?'

This time the leaders didn't answer, as they were beginning to feel a little dizzy. 'What do you want?' said the U.S. President.

'I just want you to fear our power,' said Mooney. 'Well, actually, let us take a tour around the World now.'

Consciously, the seven leaders climbed onto Reddash with the four youngsters. The red cloth then flew slowly over waters and plains, mountains and valleys, cities and villages, and finally landed on a high grassland where colourful flowers grew. 'You see how beautiful our World is?' said Mooney. 'How can you bare the loss of such a wonderful place? And did you see the microscopic dots when you looked down from our cloth? Those were people! We all look the same from above, scattering all over the World like tiny grains of dust. Does yourself, a single being, really matter that much?'

'We ask you to work for the good of the World, and stop wars that do nothing but generate hate,' said Sherlyn. 'Promise us, and we won't bother you again.'

128

The Mission of Mooney Rooney

'Now we shall take you back home,' said Mooney. 'And do consider the deal!'

The seven leaders lowered their heads and spoke nothing.

The President of China went over to Mooney. 'Do you have time to come to my place and tell me more about your story?' he said.

Mooney smiled. 'Sorry, Mr. President,' he said. 'I only hope that you will trust us and to try your best to defend Valeor. Now we have still got important errands to run – come ride with us!'

After taking all the leaders back to their residences, the four youngsters took a deep breath. 'Now,' said Mooney, 'let us go home.'

Chapter 18
Home

Dr. Ince had already arrived in a hotel in Vancouver. He had prepared cheques for the youngsters to bring home, except for Colin who didn't tell him much about his family other than the fact that his parents were dead and that he didn't want to go home. Today, the youngsters went to see Dr. Ince in the hotel and took away the cheques.

Mooney, Sherlyn, and Jing didn't want to go home straight away, because they wanted to know if their parents really care about them. So they had decided to sit on Reddash and peep in to their houses before they went in, and Colin had agreed to do the favour for them.

The four youngsters came first to Mooney's house and saw from the windows that Mooney's parents were having dinner together.

'I called Ince today,' said Mrs. Rooney, 'but his assistant said he's gone away for a couple of days.'

'Did you ask for his cell phone number?' said Mr. Rooney.

'He wouldn't give it to me,' said Mrs. Rooney. 'Mooney's been gone for more than a month now, George. I'm worried about him.'

Mr. Rooney pointed at the newspaper he was holding in his hands. 'You know, the prices of the properties in town are going up and up and up,' he said. 'Life is getting tough.'

130

The Mission of Mooney Rooney

'Are you even listening to me?' said Mrs. Rooney. 'You don't even care about Mooney, do you?'

'He's gone for good,' said Mr. Rooney. 'He's learning how to live by himself – isn't that great? In addition, he is bringing home money.'

'All you care about is money, George!' said Mrs. Rooney. 'Our son is gone and we don't even know where he is. That Ince might be lying to us – oh god! How come I never thought of that before? What if he really lied to us? Oh...' And she started crying.

'Dr. Ince has already given us ten thousand dollars,' said Mr. Rooney, 'so, he can't be lying. Don't think too much, Chelsy; Mooney's going to come back soon.'

Sitting outside of the house, Mooney showed no particular emotions regarding his parent's conversation. 'Let's go,' he said.

They came to Sherlyn's house. It was Sherlyn's brother Paul's birthday, and the family was having a party with some relatives. Having a bottle of beer, Sherlyn's father was enjoying conversations with his own siblings, while Sherlyn's mother was busy serving the guests.

'Give it back!' cried Paul. 'My sister's going to beat you up when she comes back!'

'Oh yeah?' said Paul's little cousin Dan. 'Who says she's coming back at all? She's never gonna come back, idiot!'

Paul started to cry. 'Mom!' he shouted. 'Is Sherlyn ever coming back?'

'Oh yeah, Kevin,' said Paul's uncle, 'where's your daughter?'

'Ha! How would I know?' said Sherlyn's dad. 'Hey, Sherlyn's mom! Tell your daughter to come downstairs!'

Sherlyn's mother gave him a glare. 'She's been gone for a month already, didn't you know that?' she said.

'Where's she gone to?' asked Sherlyn's aunt.

131

'How would I know?' said Sherlyn's dad.

Sherlyn sighed. 'Let's get out of here,' she said.

On the way to his house, Jing hesitated. 'Sorry guys,' he said, 'I think I'm not going back at the moment.'

'Why not?' asked Sherlyn.

'Because I know what they'll say,' said Jing, 'and I don't want to hear it. My parents always like to hide their real feelings and speak harshly about me. You won't understand...I just don't want to go back yet.'

Mooney sighed. 'Okay then,' he said. 'Let's go back to find Mr. Chubby.'

Dr. Ince saw the youngsters and was glad. 'Come on,' he said. 'Let's go downstairs and have a buffet dinner!'

For the following couple of days, Colin was content to stay with Dr. Ince, while the others had decided to go home and say goodbye to their families.

*   *   *

In the evening, Jing's parents got home from work and saw that their son was sitting quietly on the couch in the living room. Jing's mother stopped at the door and said, 'You're back! How come you didn't tell us that you're coming back tonight? Oh let me look at you...have you gone any thinner? Was the game any fun?'

'Mom...'

'You've finally completed it son,' said Jing's father. 'Now shall we have dinner?'

'I've had dinner already,' said Jing. 'Oh, and here's the prize I got from the game...I was the champion, basically. Here, take it.'

'Wow!' cried Jing's mother. 'One hundred thousand American!'

'Dad,' said Jing, 'can you take a day off tomorrow? I want to spend some time with you and mom.'

132

The Mission of Mooney Rooney

'I'll see,' said his dad, smiling. 'I can't just take a day off too suddenly.'

'You should go to sleep now, son, if you've had dinner already. It's getting late,' said Jing's mom.

The next morning, Jing came downstairs and saw that his parents were waiting for him at the kitchen table. 'We've both taken a day off today,' said his dad, 'and we're going to take you around town. We haven't seen too much of Vancouver yet, have we?'

Jing smiled and sat in front of his breakfast. 'Mom, I want to ask you something,' he said.

'Go ahead,' she said.

'Do you believe in God?'

'Well, sometimes yes, sometimes no,' she said. 'But most of the time I believe that God exists. And I hope for His salvation to come.'

'Do you believe Him only because you want salvation?' said Jing.

'Why, son?' said his father. 'You talk strangely today.'

'Do you believe in heaven, dad?' said Jing.

'As you know, I'm slightly Buddhist,' said his father. 'The Buddhist heaven is different from the heaven we normally talk about, and you have to come into Buddhahood to enter the Buddhist heaven. I suppose you haven't learned much in the Shaolin Temple other than Kung Fu, eh?'

'But dad, do you believe in God?' said Jing.

'Son, the most important thing is not what you believe in,' said his dad, 'but is what you get from what you believe in. For example, fortune? Peace at heart?'

'Does that really matter?' said Jing.

'What are you talking about son?' said his mom.

'Oh,' said Jing. 'I mean if you believe in something, go ahead and believe it. And if you don't believe in something, then don't. You shouldn't be looking for anything in return.'

'Let's not talk about this topic,' said his dad. 'Let's see: we're going to have lunch in Steveston, and then go to Granville Island and Stanley Park...'

Sitting in his dad's car, Jing attempted to speak several times, but since he didn't know what to say, he spoke nothing after all. He knew that he had to leave tomorrow, but he wasn't sure if he was going to return.

In the evening, the family was having dinner at a Chinese restaurant in Richmond.

'Dining with your family is the most blissful thing in life!' said Jing's dad.

Immediately Jing's eyes turned red. 'Dad,' he said, 'I have to go tomorrow.'

'What?' said both of his parents at the same time.

'I signed a contract with the program, that I have to enter the final competition for a world title,' said Jing. 'I'm going to compete with people from all over the world.'

'But you have to go, do you?' said his mom.

Jing didn't answer.

'Well, if you've signed the contract already, you have to go,' said his dad. 'It's important that we keep the promises that we make. When will you return this time? School's going to start soon, you know. Do you want me to give you a ride to the where you need to go tomorrow?'

'It's okay,' said Jing. 'Some of the staff will come pick me up.'

'Now eat more then, son,' said his mom. 'Eat more while you still can.'

The next morning, Jing woke up early and watched his parents drive away for work. He bid them farewell, and blessed them from the bottom of his heart.

* * *

The Mission of Mooney Rooney

'Mom, mom! Sherlyn is back!' Paul rushed to give a big hug his sister.

'Hey mom,' said Sherlyn, 'I'm back.'

'Aw girl I've been missing you,' said Mrs. Claxton. 'Come on in for dinner.'

'I already had dinner,' said Sherlyn. 'Here…is one hundred thousand dollars.'

Her mother cried out in joy. 'You did it, Sherlyn! I know you would be the champion! Well you've always been good at sport, and this competition shouldn't have been hard for you eh? But take the money back. If your dad sees it, he's going to spend it all in less then an hour, you know.'

'Just keep it for yourself, mom,' said Sherlyn. 'Buy something for yourself and Paul. Or maybe for daddy too.' She took a deep breath. 'I have to leave again in a couple of days for the final title.'

'What? You're leaving again?' said Mrs. Claxton.

'Yeah. I've signed a contract with them,' said Sherlyn.

In the evening, Sherlyn's father came home and saw that her stepdaughter was back. But he didn't show any surprise and had dinner just as usual. Suddenly Sherlyn asked, 'Mom, do you believe in God?'

'Of course,' said her mom. 'You know I pray everyday.'

'Why do you believe?' said Sherlyn.

'I've been telling you since you were small,' said Mrs. Claxton, 'that God created and loves us. Anyone who believes in him will have eternal life.'

'What if there was no eternal life?' said Sherlyn. 'Would you still believe in him?'

Mrs. Claxton hesitated. 'I haven't thought of that,' she said. 'But I think…once you believe in him, you'll have eternal life…? I never doubted that.'

Sherlyn's dad laughed. 'I'm not that idealistic,' he said. 'I don't care if I go to heaven or not. I only want to be happy in the rest of my life, that's it. And I don't even care if I go to hell.'

'Don't say that in front of the kids,' said Mrs. Claxton.

'You all value yourselves on top of everything,' said Sherlyn in a low voice.

So the family didn't speak anymore for the evening.

Mrs. Claxton couldn't see a reason to tell her husband that Sherlyn was leaving again soon. The next day, Sherlyn stayed at home all day and lived just as usual with her family. As she watched her mom keeping in the backyard and her brother playing video games happily by himself, she silently bid them farewell, and blessed them from the bottom of her heart.

* * *

Coming home from work in the evening, Mrs. Rooney heard the familiar sound of Mooney's piano. 'Mooney, is that you?' she said softly.

When Mooney got home, the first thing he did was hopping on to his piano seat. He lifted up the lid and started to press his fingers on his old friend – piece after piece he played, until he had forgotten about the whole World. 'Mooney!' cried Mrs. Rooney. Mooney jerked off from his piano and ran to give his mother a hug.

'Do you want to give dad a phone call?' said Mrs. Rooney.

'It's okay,' said Mooney. 'He should be on his way home.'

'I don't think so,' said Mrs. Rooney. 'He's having a late meeting tonight – he won't be back till midnight. Um…I have to go out tonight too…do you want to come with me?'

'Nah,' said Mooney. 'It's okay, mom.'

'I'm going to auntie Helen's,' said Mrs. Rooney.

The Mission of Mooney Rooney

'I'll just stay at home,' said Mooney.

'Okay then...here's fifty dollars. Go buy yourself dinner,' said Mrs. Rooney, who then ran upstairs to her room.

'Mom, I got something to ask you,' yelled Mooney at the bottom of the stairs.

'I don't have time now – ask me tomorrow okay?' yelled Mrs. Rooney.

So Mooney stayed home with his piano for the rest of the night.

The next morning, Mooney woke up at seven and went downstairs for breakfast. He saw a note on the table saying:

Mooney, dad didn't come home last night. I have an early meeting today: there's food for you in the fridge. Dad and I will come back for dinner with you. Mom.

Mooney sat down and said nothing.

In the evening, Mrs. Rooney came back early with lots of Mooney's favourite food. 'You must have eaten very little during that competition eh?' said Mrs. Rooney. 'Dad has postponed his meeting tonight and he should be coming back soon.'

Mooney sat at the kitchen table and watched his mother preparing for dinner. He had never paid much attention to her before; now as he looked at her, he found that she was indeed very beautiful, and that she loved him very much. So he got up and held his mother by her waist.

'What's the matter?' said Mrs. Rooney, who turned around and kissed him on his forehead.

'I have to go tomorrow,' said Mooney.

'Eh what?' said Mrs. Rooney. 'Oh! My chicken...'

Mr. Rooney came home at eight o'clock that evening. 'Mooney!' he said. 'Sorry to have kept you waiting!'

Finally, the family had dinner together again, but they didn't talk much. Suddenly Mrs. Rooney remembered something.

'Mooney, did you have something to ask me last night?' she said.

'Oh yeah,' said Mooney. 'Um…dad, do you believe in God?'

'Well,' said Mr. Rooney, 'I believe that God is there, but I don't believe that God can help us. I rely on myself.'

'Mooney,' said Mrs. Rooney, 'God is always there with you, and He plans everything out for you. Do rely on Him.'

'God exists,' said Mooney, 'but he doesn't exist for us. Whether you believe in Him or not, he is there. And we won't receive any reward from believing.'

'Okay, whatever you say, you've got to try this tonight,' said Mrs. Rooney, who got up and took some pork ribs out of the oven.

That night, Mooney didn't say a word about having to leave. Waking up the next morning, he saw nobody at home and wrote a note, saying:

Mom, dad: I'm sorry that I have to leave again for the final competition. Here's a cheque of one hundred thousand American dollars. I hope you'd take it. I will come back before school starts. Don't worry about me, and please take care. Mooney.

Blessing his parents from the bottom of his heart, Mooney put down his pen reluctantly. Walking out of the front door with his backpack, he was all ready for another journey.

* * *

Colin had had a great time in town with Dr. Ince. The two of them went to a lot of places: PNE, Science World, the Aquarium, and sushi restaurants. Since his parents died, Colin had never had so much

The Mission of Mooney Rooney

fun before. Being with Dr. Ince, he seemed to have forgotten all about the unhappy things that he had gone through. Today, the three other youngsters joined Colin and Dr. Ince in the hotel. 'It's time to go,' said Mooney.

'Do you need help on anything?' said Dr. Ince.

'No, thanks,' said Mooney. 'You've done a lot for us already, and we really don't know how thank you. The only thing you have to do now is to wait for us to come back. And if we don't show up after too long, you'll know what to do…right?'

Noticing the tears in Mooney's eyes, Dr. Ince lowered his head and looked at Colin, who said, 'You've been like a father to me, Mr. Chubby…' and tears rushed out of his eyes.

Dr. Ince held him close. 'When you come back,' he said, 'I shall be your father, if you may take my offer.'

Chapter 19
Ündia

According to what Muloka had said, the Valeoran-Ündian Leap Hole nearest to Vancouver was located in Banff, Alberta. Renowned for its beauty, Banff was a major tourist attraction in Western Canada. As Reddash lingered above the small town, Mooney took out the Leap Hole detecting device Muloka had given him and listened to its signal. Muloka said that this Leap Hole was going to open at noon, and if the youngsters missed it, they had to wait for another twelve hours for it to open again.

As they came above a famous coffee shop, the beeping of the device became more frequent. It was at about 11:55am when the four of them went inside the coffee shop searching for the exact location of the Leap Hole. The device gave out a long beep when they came to a table in the corner of the shop; all the people in the shop looked strangely at them, and Mooney had no choice but to turn off the device. The table was occupied by four ladies, who were sitting deep in conversation and had no signs of leaving.

'It's about noon,' said Jing. 'If they don't go away, they'll be sucked into the Leap Hole with us.'

The Mission of Mooney Rooney

'Not everyone can fall into Leap Holes,' said Mooney. 'Only special people can. These ladies would be sitting there just fine, but the problem is that we have to stand exactly where they are in order to go to Ündia.'

'Come on! It's two minutes to twelve!' said Sherlyn.

Cockroaches were the most abundant and hated insects in the world, and to Mooney, they were the most useful creatures in this kind of situations. So, as he sang in a low voice, more than ten small cockroaches climbed onto the legs of the four ladies, who immediately jumped up from their seats, knocked down their table and ran around mad inside the coffee shop. 'Now!' said Sherlyn.

The four youngsters then stood at where the table were. Holding hands, they formed a circle and closed their eyes – when the clock struck twelve, they were gone. Busy rescuing the four ladies from cockroach attack, the people in the coffee shop didn't see what happened to the youngsters at all.

*　*　*

After feeling like being squeezed, the four youngsters landed on something and felt extremely hot. As they opened their eyes, they saw that they were lying on a piece of bare rock, and that something was flowing slowly like blood below them. It was lava – hot lava! The flow of lava was so great that it looked like a river, and the rock they were lying on was like a small island in the middle of the river. Despite their ability to withstand heat, the four of them could still feel hot on the rock.

As they looked around them, they realized that they were inside a huge rock tunnel which was lighted up by the flowing lava below. Steam was coming up from the lava, obscuring the vision of the youngsters.

'We can't stay here any longer!' said Jing.

'Let's use Reddash,' said Sherlyn.

As Colin took out Reddash, he felt that there was something wrong with this place. And when the four youngsters sat on the cloth, they sank slowly in the air along with Reddash. 'What's wrong?' asked Mooney.

'I don't know,' said Colin. 'Perhaps the air here is less dense.'

'Anyway, let's fly around and see if there's any opening to this tunnel,' said Mooney. However, Reddash flew like a fly and hit itself blindly on the wall of the rock tunnel.

'We can try following the direction of where the lava is flowing,' said Sherlyn.

So Colin did what she said. But the speed of Reddash was unexpectedly slow. 'Can we go faster?' said Jing. 'We're about to melt.'

'I've try many times and this is the fastest we can go,' said Colin.

'Fly steady,' said Mooney.

Suddenly, a slender object shot out from the lava below. Hissing and carrying fresh magma, the creature was about three feet long, diving head on to the youngsters. Luckily Reddash was quick enough to dodge away from its attack, and the creature hit nothing and dropped back to the flowing lava.

'What the heck was that thing?' said Sherlyn.

All at once, several more of those things shot out from the lava and came to Reddash in all directions. Jing immediately took out his stick and whacked at one of the things – the creature hissed and was sliced into half, but the heat from it was so strong that it travelled though the stick and burned Jing's hand. Paying no heed to the pain, Jing continued to strike down the upcoming creatures until none was left in the path of Reddash.

As Jing sat down in relief, a knoll emerged from the lava in front of Reddash. As the knoll increased in height, the youngsters opened their mouths and saw a giant snake, a giant red snake with horns on

142

its head, scales on its body and wing-like fins on its back. As it gave out its horrible cry, fire rushed out of its mouth and came straight to Reddash.

'It's all you now, Colin!' cried Sherlyn.

Colin grabbed tightly onto Reddash, which nimbly avoided the incoming flames. Despite the fact that the cloth was a lot slower than before, it was still capable of flying at a great speed relative to any other things. So in a few seconds, Reddash survived through the flames and speeded across the monster, which immediately lifted its entire body out of the lava and flew directly after the cloth. At this moment, the youngsters noticed that the air was becoming easier for them to breathe – they had taken the right direction and were coming near the end of the tunnel.

'That thing is fast!' said Jing. 'Come on Colin! You can do it!'

Once again, the giant snake blew out its flame. As Reddash was about to be consumed by the fire, the cloth became greater in speed near the opening of the tunnel, launching out just in time to escape from the malice of the monster.

As the youngsters turned back and looked, they saw that the opening of the tunnel was located on the wall of a cliff that was about several hundred feet high, and that the lava was pouring out slowly from the cave to form a huge magmafall on the cliff. Flying out of the tunnel, the giant red snake gave out a wailing cry and fell off the cliff. As it hit the rocks below, its body broke apart like a carbon rod, and was dead.

'Can't it fly?' said Jing.

'I guess it's because of the temperature difference between here and inside the tunnel,' said Sherlyn.

'Yeah,' said Mooney. 'I can feel a little cold out here.'

For the atmosphere was crowded with thick, grey clouds, the youngsters could see little sunlight as they lifted up their heads to the sky. And as they looked down, they saw that the endlessly pouring magma from the mountain had formed a great river that flowed in winds through a big forest, and that the plants near the river were all black, burned to death. The forest looked dark green from above, while no flowers of any sort could be seen.

'I believe that we're in Ündia now,' said Sherlyn. 'So, what's next?'

Before Mooney could answer, a clan of birds flew out of nowhere and was looking extremely aggressive. Colin immediately accelerated his cloth and tried to escape, but Reddash still couldn't reach its usual speed in the open air of Ündia. As the birds came closer, the youngsters saw that they resembled crows, except that they were gigantic in size and had teeth inside their red beaks which looked like the mouths of lions. Since the attack of the birds was so organized, the youngsters were quickly surrounded. 'Into the forest below!' cried Mooney.

'But it seems unsafe down there,' said Sherlyn.

'We have no choice,' said Mooney.

Dodging away from the birds below it, Reddash dived straight into the forest. The youngsters held on tight to the cloth as they strode through the canopies; finally, they landed safely on a thick yellow leaf as big as a boat on the forest floor. The youngsters sat and heard that the birds did not enter the forest – the creatures screeched, lingered above the trees for a moment and were gone.

The forest floor was packed with huge fallen leaves, looking like a carpet that covered almost half the height of the trees. As the youngsters looked up, they saw very little light coming from above; with tree trunks that stood like giant pillars, the forest itself looked like a large gloomy hall, where the youngsters were sitting on its carpet listening to their own breaths.

'Colin,' said Sherlyn panting, 'we don't know where we're going yet. So don't move.'

144

'I'm not moving,' said Colin. At once Mooney realized something and whispered, 'There's something below the leaves!'

So Colin elevated Reddash a little and let it fly low above the fallen leaves. Suddenly, something stirred and hissed in front of them, and a black thing emerged from the deep sea of leaves below. Although there wasn't much light, the youngsters could still see that it was a head of a monster.

'Darn,' said Sherlyn. 'It's a snake again!'

At once Reddash sprang back. But another massive scaly thing revealed itself from the leaves right below Reddash and knocked the youngsters out of the cloth. Luckily, the four of them landed on the thing and jumped back to Reddash in several summersaults.

'That's the body of the snake,' said Sherlyn. 'Let's try flying sideways.'

So Colin did as she said. But after a few seconds, another snakehead popped up from the leaves, followed quickly by another...

'It's too dangerous here,' said Mooney. 'We have to fly out of the forest!'

'But there're birds outside,' said Jing.

'Try flying to the magma river!' cried Sherlyn.

So Reddash launched out of the forest and flew low above the top canopy. Noticing the reappearance of their target, the horrifying birds came out of their hidings and began their hunt again. However, they didn't come any nearer to them, seemingly to be afraid of the black snakes, which were shooting their heads out of the canopy for attack. With danger hanging loosely above and below them, the youngsters flew hastily toward the magma river.

As they reached the river, they found that the snakes as well as the birds shrieked and wouldn't get near. 'Looks like they're all scared of the heat,' said Jing.

'Then let's stay as close to the magma as we can,' said Sherlyn.

'But we don't know how long this river is and where it leads to,' said Mooney.

'We can't care too much now,' said Jing. 'Just lie on your back and look at those stupid birds above!'

After a while of flight, Mooney took out another Aetherian device from his backpack. It was a square pyramid mounted on top of a cube; on each sides of the pyramid there was an impression of a palm print. 'Let's refill some of our energy while we're still safe,' said Mooney. As the youngsters put their palms onto the impressions on the four surfaces respectively, they could feel a stream of energy that rushed through their arms and into their bodies. In this way, they didn't have to eat for as long as ten days.

The flight continued. 'Do you feel something in the air that's sort of strange?' said Mooney.

'Yeah,' said Sherlyn. 'I feel a bit hard to breathe. Muloka said that the contents in the air of Ündia are different from the other two Worlds. I think that's why Reddash is flying slower than ever.'

'Would the air be bad for our health, then?' asked Jing.

'How would I know?' said Mooney, smiling. 'Didn't you pay attention to Muloka's lessons? He said that Ündia is very different from Valeor in many ways. For example, the Aetherian insect scouts can always return from Valeor with useful information, but few of them can survive going back from Ündia. In this way, what Aetherians know about Ündia is little. But they do know that the Ündians cannot live outside or in the natural environment, just like the Aetherians. Yet they do not know where they live.'

'They mustn't be in caves,' said Colin, 'since there is lava in the mountains. And they don't live on ground…where else could they dwell?'

146

The Mission of Mooney Rooney

'Underwater?' said Jing.

Abruptly, the magma river widened. Since the birds had given up their chase, the youngsters could fly higher now for a better view. They saw in front of them a large mass of steam, and water – it was an ocean, they thought. They found a beach nearby and landed there.

Getting off from Reddash, the four of them walk on the pink sand of the beach and looked toward the horizon across the sea. They lifted their heads and saw that the sun was dim among the dark clouds, and that the sea was silent and serene. Ündia was indeed a strange yet beautiful World.

'Is this a sea or a lake?' asked Sherlyn suddenly. 'If it's a sea, then how come there're no waves? If it's a lake, then how come we can't see the other side of the shore? This is for sure too big to be a lake.'

'Normally, waves in a sea are generated by wind,' said Mooney. 'But as you can see here, the air is so still. It's for sure not strong enough to make waves.'

'We can taste the water and see if it's a sea or a lake,' said Colin. So Mooney and Sherlyn dipped their hands into the water.

'Wait!' cried Jing. 'The water might be poisonous!'

Mooney and Sherlyn retracted their hands together. 'Thanks, Jing,' said Mooney. 'I haven't thought of that. Well, it doesn't matter if it's a sea or a lake. We'll just say for now that it's a lake.'

'Look!' said Colin suddenly, pointing to the centre of the lake.

The others looked and saw nothing. 'What is it Colin?'

'There're bubbles coming up from the water!' said Colin.

Sherlyn smiled. 'That's normal, Colin,' she said. 'When animals breathe underwater...'

Animals! Sherlyn looked at Mooney immediately. 'Would it be...?'

'Would it be a giant snake again?' said Jing. 'Gee, how I hate those things!'

They laughed. 'Let's go take a look,' said Mooney. 'Perhaps the Ündians live down there.'

But Colin hesitated. 'I think someone's watching us.'

The youngsters then turned around but could find nothing suspicious. 'Just be careful, and we'll be okay,' said Mooney. He then took out another Aetherian device from his backpack – this time a rod with some buttons of different colours on it. 'This thing can create protection capsules,' said Mooney. 'Once we put ourselves into one of these capsules, we can wander around safely in water.'

Mooney then pointed the rod at Jing and pressed the green button on it. Slowly, from the hole on its end, the rod blew out a bubble big enough to engulf Jing, who touched the transparent surface of the capsule from the inside and said it was elastic. But the others couldn't hear him, for the capsule can absorb any sound – the youngsters had to communicate with their bodies instead. Now, having all surrounded by individual capsules, the youngster were ready to dive into the water.

They jumped into the "lake" by leaping some twenty yards away from the beach, and they moved toward where the bubbles came from. Striding through the dark water, they saw no fish or living things of any kind; as they continued to dive, they wondered why they couldn't see the bottom of this "lake" – perhaps it was very much deeper than they had imagined.

So they continued their journey underwater, until they saw many faint spots of light below them and were excited. But Mooney told the others to calm down and to follow him in single file: so Colin moved closely behind him, followed by Sherlyn and Jing, who turned around now and then to see if there was anything behind them.

As they came closer to the spots of light, the youngsters halted. They looked down and saw something so stunning that they could never forget in their lives – it was a city, a real, living, city underwater!

Chapter 20
The City under Water

The city under water had no bound. The youngsters could see no boundaries other than its edge below them. They saw that there were colonies of buildings packed neatly on the floors of the city, and that there was light shining through the walls of each building, brightening up the whole city. There were places among the buildings which were letting out a massive amount of bubbles that were seeking their way up to the surface of the water – these were probably the bubbles the youngsters saw from the beach.

While the four of them were looking at the city in wonder, there appeared more than ten beings from behind, who quickly surrounded them. These beings looked like human – they had a head and four limbs. However, every inch of their bodies except the regions around their eyes and mouths was covered by dark, green scales. Now Jing had put his hands on his stick, but Mooney told him to calm down, for he saw that the scaly men carried no weapons in their hands and should mean no harm.

One of the scaly men made some signals to the youngsters with his hands, seemingly to be expecting an answer from them. Sherlyn watched the signals and thought that the men might very possibly be attempting to take them into the city. So she made some signals with her hands, too – at once the man dived down, while the rest of the men formed two lines on the sides of the youngsters and escorted them to the lakebed.

As they sank to the bottom of the lake, they saw that the wall surrounding the edge of the city was transparent – they could hardly detect the presence of the wall at first. But they could see through the wall that the floor panel of the city was more than sixty feet deep; the wall itself was lined by a huge circular tube that had an opening at its bottom. As the youngsters moved to the water below the tube, they felt that their bodies were floating up involuntarily to the opening. They had entered the city, and had also made a huge discovery – the inside of the tube was not water, but a piece of dry land. It was air that filled the huge space inside the floor panel. Mooney remembered a science demonstration done by his elementary school teacher, that if you put a finger on top of a test tube, turn it upside-down and put it into water, the air inside the tube remains there even after you pull away your finger. It seemed that the Ündians had integrated this property of nature into their lives.

Mooney took out the Aetherian rod device, pressed the red button on it and recycled all the capsules into the rod. Until the whole escort had entered the city, some of the scaly men stood before a thing that looked like a small railway track. At once a metal plate appeared underneath their feet and moved them onto the track. The four youngsters did the same thing, and were soon gliding swiftly on the track with the team of scaly men. In fact, all the people in the city travelled along these tracks on this "basement" level, where all entrances of buildings were located.

After a while, the metal plates slowed down as they got near a building. Two of the scaly men walked to the entrance, waved their hands at the door and opened it. The youngsters were then led into the entrance space, which moved upwards like an elevator. Abruptly, the elevator stopped, and the youngsters had reached one of the higher levels in the building.

The walls of this building were all clear like glass, and the youngsters could overlook the bright city from the level they were on. They saw that most of the other buildings were made out of the same glass-like materials; with light shining through the walls of the buildings, the city looked like a giant collection of beautiful sparkling diamonds. Other than the view, the youngsters also noticed that there were vertical rod-like structures standing around the room. These rods were about three feet tall, and on top of each there was a big marble that gave out white light. Seemingly, the whole room was lighted up by these glowing marbles on the rods.

Suddenly a man approached them – they turned around and were shocked. This man was wearing a wrinkled long robe and a waist belt, both made out of dried sea plants. Having long, dark hair, the man let out a smile through his beard. 'Hello,' said the Valeoran man politely. 'My name is Rich, Richard Barton, and I am from America. Don't be afraid – this place is totally safe.'

But Mooney didn't trust him, for the scaly men had begun to seize the backpacks from the youngsters. Sherlyn and Jing were all ready to attack. 'Sagguru,' said the Valeoran man, and at once the scaly men entered the elevator and left.

'Okay, now,' said Rich. 'I hope you'd feel more comfortable without those men around you.' He sat on the ground and told the youngsters to do the same. 'Do you know each other?'

Mooney nodded.

Rich sighed. 'Every time when people come here, those scaly men would bring them to me,' said Rich. 'I know I'm not the first visitor here, but I've been living here for almost fifty years.' The youngsters looked at him again in astonishment.

Rich smiled. 'I was about fifty years old when I got here,' he said, 'so now I should be a hundred years old. But the growth rate in this place is rather low, so, I look as though I'm about sixty, do I not? Since I'm a language genius, I picked up their language very soon, and the scaly men used me as an interpreter every time when people like you come visit. That's basically what I do here.'

Seemingly, the scaly people didn't know what the youngsters were here for – they brought them to Rich, thinking that they were ordinary Valeorans who dropped through a Leap Hole by accident.

'The natives here are pretty much the same as we are, except that they have scales instead of skin,' said Rich. 'I've asked them about their scales, and they said that their forefathers once had skin and lived on shore. But because of the lack of sunlight in the environment, the air became loaded with many unknown substances, which generated a common skin disease among the people. This disease caused them to itch all the time, and they had to place their bodies in water in order to feel better. Time after time, the disease progressed into a mutation, which turned the skin into a rough layer of scale-like bumps. So, for convenience's sake, the people just moved into the water to live. I always hear the scaly people saying: "It's not fair! If everything's by chance, then why does it have to be us? Why – why was there chance in the first place? It's not fair!"

'I don't really understand what they mean, but who cares? Well, now, since you've come already, please take time to get yourselves to feel at home.'

'Rich,' said Sherlyn, 'where…or what exactly is this place?'

Rich laughed. 'I have no clue!' he said. 'Even after fifty years, I still have no idea about where and what this place is. Well, sometimes I

The Mission of Mooney Rooney

think it is a small hidden corner on the Earth, and sometimes, I think it is another world apart from our own!'

Mooney looked at him with sympathy. 'What did you do as a living before you came here?' He asked.

'Oh, I was a scientist,' said Rich. 'I got into space research after fighting for America in WWII, and I came to this place shortly after that. During the past fifty years of my stay here, I got to know a little about modern space technology from other visitors, and I'm feeling proud for my own country.'

'Did you say that there are other visitors?' said Sherlyn.

'Yeah…there are no more than twenty of them,' said Rich. 'And as far as I know, they all live in this city.'

'What do the scaly people keep you here for?' asked Sherlyn.

'Well, they mean no harm,' said Rich. 'They just want us to do something for them, and they don't care much about what we do for the rest of the time. They say that when they don't need us anymore, they'll send us back home.' And Rich looked at Colin and sighed. 'This is the first time I see people so young like you coming here,' he said. 'Well, don't worry – I believe that you'll go home someday – we all will, indeed. Now get up and follow me!'

The five of them went to the level in the building where the other visitors dwelled. Walking along the corridor, the youngsters saw that the faces of the visitors were all grave as stones, and that their movements were dry and rigid as they came out of the doors and waved their hands at the newcomers. Most of them were wearing the same kind of clothes as Rich, while a few of them were in tattered Valeoran clothes, seemingly to be burdened by weariness of boredom and despair.

'Rich,' said Colin, 'these people look…scary.'

Rich smiled. 'Don't be scared,' he said. 'We're all on the same boat.'

153

'Do we have to wear clothes like yours?' asked Sherlyn.

'No,' said Rich; 'not yet. The clothes you're wearing are still new. Since the scaly people don't wear clothes, we have to make them for ourselves. The best material for clothing here is this kind of sea plant.'

'This village looks pretty big,' said Mooney: 'huge for a group of less than twenty. But the design looks plain and primitive. Did the scaly people build it for you?'

'Yes, they did,' said Rich. 'Those scaly people have high intelligence and don't behave like us most of the time – they do things only for the sake of their basic needs. So when we first came here, we felt very dull without all the colourful things we've had in our lives back then. Here's a total lack of colour. But if you think deeper, there's no need for colour.'

'That's not true,' said Colin. 'Existence is different from living.'

Rich looked at Colin for a long time but didn't speak.

'I've been noticing those glowing marbles,' said Mooney. 'Are those the city's main source of light?'

'Yeah,' said Rich. 'Those are some refined minerals that the scaly people discovered from the lakebed. If you heat up one of those marbles, it gives out light; when it wears out, you reheat it again.'

'How do you heat up the marbles?' asked Mooney.

'Oh, we have many ways to do that,' said Rich. 'For example, we can put the marbles near flowing lava. Or, since we have lightning here very often, the scaly people have developed a technology to collect the energy from lightning and use it as a power source. If we could do this in our old home, that would be great, wouldn't it?'

Jing laughed. 'There's not much lightning in Valeor,' he said.

'What?' said Rich. 'What Valeor?'

At once Jing and Sherlyn looked at Mooney. 'Um…Valeor means our old home,' said Mooney.

154

The Mission of Mooney Rooney

Rich could feel that the youngsters were hiding something from him. 'Oh, okay,' he said. 'Anyway, you can tell me more about yourselves after you get to know me more. Here now, this is your room: you can all live in a single room if you want, since you're kids. And I've made some furniture here myself for newcomers – go in and have a look!'

The four of them went inside and saw some plain, old-fashioned furniture sitting at the corners of the room – it's good enough for everyday needs. The youngsters were very much gratified.

Looking out of the transparent walls, Sherlyn said, 'This city under water is really beautiful. If there was fish around, that'd be perfect.'

'I haven't seen a single fish like those in our old home,' said Rich. 'All we have here are some very aggressive species. So don't go into the open water – it's very dangerous. For now, please take a rest, and we'll have a welcoming feast for you later!'

In a spacious dining hall, Rich introduced the four newcomers to the other visitors, who nodded a little and spoke nothing. Some of the visitors took out some food from the kitchen and told the others to begin the feast.

Seeing the expression on the youngsters' faces, Rich laughed. 'I felt the same when I first came here; but you know, you have to get used to this anyway, because you can't survive starving.'

'What...what's that you're eating?' said Jing.

'Well, since we can't go out of the city and hunt, we have to eat what the scaly people eat,' said Rich. 'But we cook differently. For example...' He pointed at a dark-grey, globular, jelly-like object that was larger than a human head. 'This is a spider belly,' he said. 'The scaly people like to suck its content raw, but we like to eat it cooked.'

The four youngsters almost popped their eyes out. 'How come... how come there's such a large...spider?' said Jing.

'This is large?' said Rich. 'No, no. Large spiders taste bad – this is a baby spider. Um...see those slender things over there? Those are giant millipedes. We skin them first and put them into boiling salt water. You know, I've never tasted anything so delicious in my life until I got here.'

There were about twenty different main dishes on the table. The youngsters dared not to ask anymore about the food and kept their own dishes empty. Chewing a millipede, Rich said, 'I think you should try those ones over there. They are snake eggs – the scaly people go on shore and harvest them from the nests of the giant snakes. Very precious food. Oh, and these are lizard tails right here, and that one right there is a frog.' The youngsters looked and saw a grey thing as big as a basketball lying on a dish; with its belly facing the ceiling and its limbs arched, it looked as though it was saying 'hug me'.

'It's enough, Rich,' said Sherlyn. 'We're not hungry...we'll have some veggies.'

So Rich brought in front of them a bowl of vegetables. 'Hm...this tastes pretty good,' said Sherlyn. 'But it has a familiar flavour...'

'The familiar flavour of meat, is that right?' said Rich. The youngsters nodded.

'You have good taste buds,' said Rich. 'This is actually...' The youngsters froze and stopped chewing.

'Haha,' said Rich. 'This is actually a kind of plant, like celery. It looks pretty cute when it's living, you know, with its juicy trunk. Many animals eat this plant.'

'Yeah, it is a plant,' said a youth sitting next to the youngsters, hanging out a lizard tail on the corner of his mouth. 'It is a plant, but it's a plant that walks...' Before Rich could explain anything, Sherlyn covered her mouth with her hand and ran out of the dining hall.

Mooney stood up. 'Thank you very much for the feast,' he said. 'But we really aren't hungry. I guess we should go back to our room now.'

The Mission of Mooney Rooney

'Okay then,' said Rich. 'You'll get used to it sooner or later. Do you want to go sightseeing tomorrow?'

'Sure,' said Mooney. 'Now goodnight, everyone.'

Rich came to their room early the next morning. He didn't have any duty today, so he asked the youngsters if they want to have breakfast himself. But the youngsters rejected him as soon as he asked, and he wondered why they could stand so long without food.

'This city is big,' said Rich. 'What kind of places do you want to go visit?'

'Prohibited areas,' said Sherlyn. 'Uh, I mean, important places like the president's residence?'

Rich looked strangely at her. 'Why do you want to go to those places?'

'We looked out of the transparent walls from our room last night,' said Mooney immediately, 'and we only saw ordinary buildings. We're just wondering if we can go to the centre of the city, to see and admire the technology of the scaly people.'

But finally, Rich couldn't resist himself and asked, 'You four are different from other kids I've seen. Are you those kind of...genius children?'

'Yes, we are,' said Sherlyn smiling. 'The government is sponsoring us to go to university together, but we ended up in this place...well, we're very interested in high technology stuff.'

Rich sighed. 'How costly it is for your country to lose you!' he said. 'But actually, every visitor here from our old home has a rather high intelligence, and I don't know why that is.'

First, they went to the basement level of the city and hopped on to one of those metal plates again. They were amazed to see how many scaly people were gliding on the tracks without interfering with the paths of one another.

'It seems that they don't care much about our presence,' said Sherlyn. 'Do they afraid that we would escape?'

'Why would they be afraid of that?' said Rich. 'We can't leave here – we are unable to do so. Plus, they rely on us for something, so they grant us much freedom inside the city.'

'What are they doing around here?' asked Jing.

'They are a really hardworking people,' said Rich. 'No matter their age, they work with whatever abilities they have. They live like bees: work, rest, work…until they die. They work for a better future for the whole people, not for themselves.'

As they went up to the ground level by an elevator, they were completely stunned by the amazing architecture of the scaly people. They noticed that they were standing among some tall buildings, and that the whole place was covered by a great hemispheric glass shelter. 'Look at the water above us!' said Colin. 'We're like living inside a big bubble underwater!'

'There're many of these glass domes over the city,' said Rich. 'Each community is covered by one. You could hardly notice the domes when you looked down from your room, right?'

On the ground floor inside the community, the scaly people walked around freely on the streets. Now and then, they had to jump into pools located on the sides of the streets in order to ease their itch a little bit – Colin thought that the situation was similar to Valeorans going to washrooms.

Sherlyn noticed that it was very quiet on the streets. 'Why do they talk so little?' she asked Rich.

'Their language was designed for necessary communication,' said Rich. 'What they mean by necessary communication is the exchange of ideas during work. Therefore, unlike us, they have no gossips. And, can you see the sadness written all over their faces? How are they going to gossip if they're sad like this?'

Jing scratched his head. 'They all look the same,' he said. 'How can you tell?'

'You feel sadness in the air, Jing,' said Colin.

Jing turned to Sherlyn. 'Hey, let's try jumping into one of those pools together,' he said. 'They look like hot springs.'

Sherlyn paid no heed to him. 'Rich,' she said, 'this looks like a place for work. Is this the downtown of the city?'

'You can say so,' said Rich. 'This is the city's heart for scientific and technology research. I come here most often, out of interest, and I got to know quite a few of the important scientists.'

He pointed at a large building not far away and said, 'That research centre is worth seeing. It is a very interesting piece of architecture as well – it looks like a hollowed octagon from above. Let's go there now.'

But Colin saw another building opposite to the octagon structure and gazed at it. 'What's that big rod thing over there?' he asked.

Unlike the other buildings, this great pillar had no light shining through its walls. 'That's where the Lord of the city lives,' said Rich.

'Lord of the city?' said Mooney. 'Who is that?'

'I don't know him personally,' said Rich; 'I haven't even seen him before. But I know that the whole city is under his lead and control.'

Mooney looked up to the top of the building and saw a colourful halo spinning slowly above the roof. 'That halo is...?'

'It is a symbol of the Lord,' said Rich. 'I heard that it's used for some sort of communication...but I'm not quite sure. Let's go now!'

Chapter 21
The Secret of the Laboratory

At the front door of the octagonal research centre, Rich talked to the guards for a bit before leading the youngsters through the main door. A guide met them inside, and the five Valeorans followed his lead along the halls. The youngsters saw that there were big panels like mirrors that stood on their sides, and they felt dizzy as they looked into them. 'Those mirrors are some sort of surveillance,' said Rich. 'They watch everything.'

Now the guide had led them in front of a rough glass door. He waved his hand at the door which then opened. 'The hands of these people are big,' said Jing. 'Are they used for swimming?'

'No,' said Rich. 'Those are gloves that they are wearing. Really powerful gloves.'

Before Sherlyn could ask anything more about the gloves, a scaly man appeared behind the glass door. As Rich was talking to him with a big smile on his face, the man looked at the four youngsters grimly but said nothing. He dismissed the guide and told Rich to bring the youngsters in.

'How do you recognize these people?' said Jing. 'They all look the same.'

160

The Mission of Mooney Rooney

'You will recognize them sooner or later,' said Rich.

Now that the Valeorans were alone, Rich led the youngsters around the place, showing them the newest technology and introducing them to research workers. But of course, the youngsters were interested in some other things.

Suddenly Colin pulled Mooney by the sleeve. 'Over there...'

Mooney turned around and saw a coloured photograph hanging on the wall. In the photograph, there were two beings lying on their backs, one naked, and the other cut open showing its guts. Mooney was shocked to recognize that these two beings were not Valeorans or Ündians, but Aetherians! When Sherlyn and Jing saw the photo, they were equally surprised as Mooney and Colin.

'What's the matter?' asked Rich.

'Oh, nothing,' said Mooney. 'We saw that picture. It looks a little bit strange.'

'That picture?' said Rich. 'It's nothing strange or special – I've seen one of those people.'

'You've seen one of them?' shouted the four of them at the same time.

All the research workers turned to look at them, telling them to keep their voices down. Apologizing, Rich brought the youngsters to a quieter corner. 'Don't be rude,' he said. 'I saw one of those people once in this research centre, when he was being taken to a lab by a group of scaly people. I thought that he was our kind at first, and since I saw that he was struggling in pain, I went up to the scaly people who were holding him and told them to release him and let me talk to him. But to my surprise, those scaly people shouted at me and pushed me to the floor. Then I looked at the being again and saw that his hair was shaking in the air – at once I realized that he wasn't my kind. Later I heard from the scaly people that there're more of those people out there. And that's all I know.'

161

'That's all you know?' asked Sherlyn.

'Yes,' said Rich. 'It seems that you're more interested in those beings than the science research I talked to you about.'

'We're sorry, Rich,' said Mooney. 'We'll tell you more about ourselves later. For now, could you tell me where the scaly people hide those beings?'

'Where they hide them?' said Rich. 'Hm...I don't know. Well, the scaly people have always trusted me for the past fifty years, but they warn me not to get near a certain place.'

'What place?' asked Mooney immediately.

'They won't let you go there,' said Rich.

'Just tell us where it is,' said Mooney.

'Alright,' said Rich. 'Let us get out of here first, and I'll show you where it is.'

After talking to Rich, one of the research workers opened the glass door and led the Valeorans out. Making sure that nobody else was in the hall, Rich said, 'See that octagon shaped door on your left? That's the forbidden laboratory. When you go near that door, guards will appear from nowhere and seize you. So don't even think of doing anything dangerous like that. Ah, well, actually, you can't even come in to this building without me. And also, those hair-shaking beings have no concerns with us, so don't even bother doing anything stupid.'

* * *

The night after they came back from the octagonal research centre, the four youngsters decided that they were going to break in to that forbidden place, which was certain to be containing important information related to Aetherians.

'But how are we going to get in?' said Sherlyn.

'That's super easy,' said Jing. 'We become invisible and sneak in.'

162

'Hm, that's a good idea,' said Mooney.

'Um…that's probably not going to work,' said Sherlyn.

'Why?' asked Colin.

Sherlyn lowered her head. 'Because I think it's rather dangerous,' she said.

'That's not a reason!' said Colin.

Jing giggled. 'Alright, I get it,' he said. 'You can stay here while we go.' But Mooney and Colin stared strangely at him and Sherlyn and didn't understand.

'You know what?' said Jing. 'Girls are shy. And Sherlyn's a shy girl.'

'Stop it!' said Sherlyn.

'Oh,' said Mooney. 'That's okay. Um…Colin, you can stay here too then. I'll go with Jing.' Sherlyn smiled awkwardly.

'So when are we going there?' said Jing.

'Right now,' said Mooney. Then, from his backpack, he took out a round stone that was as big as his fist. He placed it on the ground between Jing and himself, put his hands before his chest and whispered something in his mouth. Slowly, the stone began to rise and spin on its own; the bodies of the two boys slowly became invisible as the stone continue to float upwards. When the stone had gone above their heads, they had become entirely invisible, but their clothes were still hanging and moving hilariously in the air. So the two of them took off their clothes and kicked them around on the ground, playing hide and seek with Colin. Sherlyn turned her back against them and blushed.

Colin picked up their clothes from the ground and folded them. Sherlyn took two black strings out of her backpack and give them to the boys. 'Tie them around your ankles,' she said, 'in this way you can always see each other.'

At the front door of the research centre, the two boys sat on the ground and waited for the chance. After a while, a scaly man walked to the door from outside and opened it: the boys followed him in. However, that man wasn't going to the forbidden lab, and so they had to sit on the floor of the hall and waited again. Just as they were about to fall asleep, the octagon-shaped door opened, and immediately the boys jumped up and ran for their chance. But two scaly men walked out from the door and stood right in their way; in less than a second, the boys dodged to the sides, slipped through the arms of the scaly men and entered the secret place just before the door closed.

The boys held each other's hand and tiptoed across the floor. There weren't too many things in the lab, but they could see several elevated platforms like surgery tables placed at the centre of the chamber, each covered by a glass lid except for one. At that one table, there stood three scaly men working on a large specimen; as expected, the specimen was an Aetherian.

Feeling that Jing's hand was trembling violently, Mooney gave a firm grip on it with his own. Turning down the noise of their breathing as best they could, the two of them sneaked to a distance of about five feet away from the table, and saw one of the scaly men taking out a metal container and pulling out a small black object from it with a pair of forceps. The man carefully moved the object to the face of the Aetherian, whose mouth was now forced open by the other two men. The Aetherian seemed to be unconscious, despite the fact that his hair was still quivering slightly in the air.

As Mooney moved closer, he finally realized what was happening to the Aetherian. But at a nervous jerk of his hand, he knocked the empty metal container off of the tray beside the table. King, kong, king…the three scaly men stopped their operation immediately and stared at the bouncing container on the floor. Not daring to move a single thread of

The Mission of Mooney Rooney

muscle in their bodies, Mooney and Jing had nothing in their minds at that moment, except for blaming their own hearts for pounding so hard and loud.

The container spun for a while on the floor and stopped. The scaly men looked around, saw nothing, and got back to work. Cautiously, they put the black snake onto the tongue of the Aetherian and poured a bottle of liquid into his mouth. After that, the three men took their surgery gloves off and pressed the red button on the side of the table: slowly, a glass lid lowered from the ceiling and covered the table. One of the men picked up the metal container from the floor and put it back onto the tray. He then spoke with the other two men and went out of the lab with them.

Mooney and Jing took a deep sigh of relief. Suddenly Jing whispered, 'Hey, come here!'

Mooney followed Jing by his string and went to another surgery table. Through the glass lid, he saw that there was another Aetherian lying unconscious on the table. Blue light-rays were directed continuously from the lid and onto the hair of the Aetherian, which was shaking violently inside the small enclosed space.

'What are they doing to them?' said Jing.

'I'm not sure,' said Mooney, who suddenly noticed a small box that glowed at the far corner of the laboratory. He ran to it and examined it; as he pressed the buttons on the sides of it, an image of an Aetherian appeared on the top surface of the glowing box – he seemed to have activated a picture slideshow. With full attention, the two boys watched the whole gallery of complicated external and internal anatomical diagrams of Aetherians, which were precisely labelled in what they believed as the scaly language.

Abruptly, the octagon-shaped door opened, and a few scaly men walked into the lab. 'Let's go now!' Mooney whispered.

165

Just before closing the door, the scaly men felt two fast strokes of wind blowing pass their shoulders. They looked around, saw nothing, and closed the door.

'Jing, are you there?' said Mooney, panting in the entrance hall.

'Of course,' said Jing in a low voice. 'I know Kung Fu after all.'

'Apparently they're doing a complete research and analysis on Aetherians,' said Sherlyn. 'But why do they do that?'

'They want to know everything about their enemy for the sake of winning every war,' said Colin

'But I don't see that there's a war going on,' said Sherlyn. 'Well, you guys saw that they were implanting things into the Aetherians, right? I think they have also invaded their thoughts by doing so.'

'Um, I think that the scaly people actually modify the Aetherians' bodies in that lab before sending them back to Aetheria,' said Mooney.

'It seems that Ündians cannot go to Aetheria,' said Sherlyn. 'But it looks like a lot of Aetherians have dropped through Leap Holes and came here.'

'Should we tell Muloka about this?' said Mooney. "I mean, if the bodies of the Ündian-Aetherians have already been modified, then–

'We can't go back to Aetheria before our mission is done,' said Jing.

'Of course not,' said Mooney. 'But I'll know what to do. Sherlyn, if you could tell Rich about our mission as soon as possible, that'd be great. We're going to need his help. Now I must leave for the shore.'

'Are you going alone – again?' said Sherlyn.

'Yeah,' said Mooney. 'It's less obvious for me to go alone.'

After Mooney had put on his backpack, the four youngsters went together to the edge of the city where they first came in. 'That's strange,' said Sherlyn. 'Nobody is on guard along the boundary.'

The Mission of Mooney Rooney

'I guess they don't expect us to escape,' said Mooney.

'But wouldn't they still need a force of defence?' said Jing.

'I can see that all Ündians are very cooperative and peaceful,' said Mooney. 'They hold a common belief in life that the Ündian race should be the best among the other two on the planet. So there should be no offences between cities, if there're any others.'

*   *   *

Inside a capsule, Mooney emerged slowly out of the water. Seeing that nobody was on shore, he quickly slid himself through the bushes behind the beach and came to an open area. He sat down on the grass and began to chant – it was yet again a nameless melody. But as his clear voice echoed across the vast fields of Ündia, it seemed to him that all had deserted him – sitting all alone in this alien land, he was so far away from home, feeling so cold, so helpless, yet so responsible. It was he himself who had chosen to take up the mission in the first place; or was it? Wasn't everything, like how the Highest had told him, planned from the very beginning?

But indeed, he wasn't alone. About a hundred of colourful rhinoceros beetles came from all directions and surrounded Mooney. Mooney then took out an Aetherian felt-pen and wrote a glowing character on each of the beetles' backs. It was a note altogether, saying:

Ündians analyze and modify bodies of Aetherians in an unknown way. Pay attention to our captives and any returning Aetherians. Mooney.

Shivering their wings and tapping their horns, the beetles seemed to be talking to Mooney like old friends. As Mooney's singing ceased, the beetles stopped moving, too, and they lay silently on the grass beside him. Not knowing how much time had gone by, the sky started to get brighter, and the beetles took flight and headed to the other side of the field across the bushes. Mooney got up and followed them. After a while, the beetles landed on the ground surrounding another insect – it was a giant Hercules beetle that was even larger than both of Mooney's palms put together. Mooney had no way to communicate with it – he had finally found what he was looking for.

Although normal insects could travel freely across Partitions, they might not be able to communicate with Aetherians – Mooney told the ordinary beetles to locate a special scout like the red butterfly. Now, having the ordinary beetles as translators, Mooney told the special beetle to lead the others to enter Aetheria to find the Master in Dectolda. Following the Hercules beetle, Mooney's trail of notes ascended like a glowing chain and disappeared into the crack of dawn. Mooney stood in confidence, for he had realized from the deeps of his heart the faith of his destiny as a Seedling of the Emissary, and as Mooney Rooney.

* * *

After saying goodbye to Mooney, the three youngsters went back to their building. But as they reached the main hall, they saw about twenty scaly men standing there waiting for them.

Rich ran to the youngsters. 'What have you done?' he said nervously. 'They say that they're going to arrest you...where's Mooney?'

Not until the youngsters could answer, six of the scaly men went up trying to grab them, and Jing took out his stick immediately and knocked them all down onto the floor. The men got up and began to generate sparkling electricity from their gloves.

'Jing, we can't win them without safety capsules,' said Sherlyn, who turned towards Rich and yelled, 'Tell them we surrender!'

The Mission of Mooney Rooney

So Rich talked to the scaly men and turned back to Sherlyn. 'They say if you want to leave, they'll let you do so tomorrow,' he said. 'But why? Why do you want to leave in such a hurry?'

But the youngsters didn't have time to answer. The scaly men grabbed them by their arms and were taking them away. 'Rich!' shouted Sherlyn. 'Come visit us if you can; and remember to bring us our backpacks!'

In a spacious chamber, the three youngsters sat together on a couch. 'What kind of a prison is this?' said Jing. 'It's so comfortable in here!'

'Everything seems good the minute before you die,' said Colin.

Sherlyn sigh. 'I wonder where Mooney is now,' she muttered. 'If he comes back, he'll be arrested too.'

'What's bad about that?' said Colin. 'The four of us should be together, no matter what happens.'

Suddenly the door opened – it was Rich. He returned the backpacks to the youngsters and said, 'Those scaly people really mean no harm to you. They just want you to work for them. If they really wanted to hurt you, they would've killed you in the hall back there. And now they're even letting me see you and bring you things.'

'Have you seen Mooney?' said Sherlyn.

'No,' said Rich. 'But I don't understand why he escaped. It's very dangerous out there, and I'm afraid–'

'Mooney won't die!' said Colin.

'How do the scaly people know where we've been?' said Jing. 'And why don't they go after Mooney and capture him too?'

'They have surveillance at the entrance of the city,' said Rich. 'But I don't know why they don't capture Mooney...perhaps it's because they think that he's probably going to die.'

Sherlyn saw that it was time. 'Rich,' she said, 'I think I'm going to tell you something important. You're a scientist, and I think you can easily understand what I'm going to say.' So she told him all about their mission.

'That's insane!' said Rich. 'But why...why do you tell me? Are you not afraid that I might betray you?'

'As you've said, we're all on the same boat,' said Sherlyn.

'Thanks for putting your trust in me,' said Rich. 'Now how may I help you?'

'Can you find out any clue of where the Hengestone might be?' said Sherlyn.

Rich frowned deeply. 'Hm...I can't think of any ways to do that,' he said. 'But the...Ündians are taking you back tomorrow, so how are you going to find the Hengestone?'

'Why are they taking us back?' asked Sherlyn.

'They say that you're all too young to work for them in the city,' said Rich. 'So they're bringing you to the final mission right a way.'

'The final mission?' asked Jing.

'I've witnessed it several times,' said Rich. 'It is a return ceremony done on shore, and it's quite scary to watch. They give you some gifts that look like jellyfish for you to bring home...hm, it's kind of like... mysterious. Translated into our own tongue, the jellyfish objects are called "spirit spheres"...'

'Spirit spheres?' said Sherlyn. 'What are they?'

'I have absolutely no clue,' said Rich.

Sherlyn lowered her head and was in thought. 'Okay,' she said. 'We will let them take us away tomorrow.'

Chapter 22
The Spirit Spheres

The next morning, the three youngsters were brought to a big rocket-launching area in the city, where ten ships were tilted to exactly forty-five degrees up of the floor. With perfectly smooth outer surfaces and outline, the milk-coloured ships looked elegant resembling huge snake eggs, except that their front ends were sharply pointed. At the rear end of each ship there was a single propeller, and in the middle section there was a clear glass cover on top of six seats, which were located inside the body of the ship.

The youngsters were all taken into one single ship. As the glass cover was about to close, Rich rushed into the launching area and asked one of the scaly men to let him sit with the youngsters.

'It's all good now,' said Rich, seating beside the youngsters. 'I'm with you.'

'Thanks, Rich,' said Jing. 'Do they use these rockets every time they go on shore?'

'Of course not,' said Rich. 'They usually swim. We're riding these because we're going somewhere far away. Remember? They can't stay aground for too long. Also, they have put a strip of "breathing plant" in

171

their mouths while they are in water. Didn't you use one of those plants when you came here?' The youngsters shook their heads.

'Oh,' said Rich. 'Now I think I know why they said you were behaving a little strange when you came here...'

As soon as all was aboard, the youngsters heard a loud exploding sound. And as they removed their hands from their ears, they had already come out of the water along with the other nine ships.

* * *

Feeling that something was moving behind him, Mooney turned around and saw nothing but a colony of small, green plants. Having bulged trunks, these plants looked like chubby babies; but Mooney had no time to pay attention to them. As he turned and headed for the lake, he heard again the same sound of movements: he looked back, and could hardly believe his eyes – the plants were following him! The plants lifted themselves out of the soil, "walked" a short distance with their roots and anchored themselves back into the ground again. Like an army, the colony of plants was slowly approaching Mooney, who were now all ready for self-defence. But the plants yielded the spot where Mooney was standing and continued their travel – seemingly, they were totally harmless. Mooney remembered the food he ate for dinner the first night he came to the city – probably these were the plants that tasted a bit like meat.

But Mooney also remembered that they were a popular food for other animals. Before he could turn and flee, a dozen creatures resembling flying ostriches came out of nowhere and began an assault on the sea of walking plants with their long wide beaks. Very soon they had noticed Mooney and were all coming at him.

Galloping at full speed, Mooney took out a small bag from his backpack. As the flying ostriches were about to seize him with their

The Mission of Mooney Rooney

beaks, Mooney grabbed a handful of red marbles and threw them at the creatures: at once their feathers caught on fire, and they fell to the ground in pain and ran for the forest. But Mooney saw a black shadow whipping amongst the trees of the forest, where the cries of the birds were ever louder – it was a giant black snake.

Mooney put himself into a capsule as he was about to reach the lake. To his surprise, he saw ten flying ships launching out of the water and were all flying in the same direction. Mooney was certain that these were the ships of the Ündians, and so he decided to run after them to see what was going on. However, he wasn't fast enough to keep up with the ships, despite having received a gift from the Highest. So he took out the Aetherian pyramid device, refilled some energy, and began a marathon towards where the ships were heading.

* * *

Over the forest, the ships were flying at a rather low speed in order to save energy in case of animal attacks. The three youngsters looked down and saw giant snakeheads popping up and down trying to sink their teeth into the ships, which were maintaining at a height just above their reach, causing them to fall back to the forest in frustration. After a while, some monster birds came from the mountains and hammered their beaks at the ships. The three youngsters saw the hideous faces of the birds and were screaming on top of their voices; but as one of the scaly men on their ship pressed a button on the control panel, the outer wall of the ship became electrically charged and knocked off the birds, which then fell through the air and into the mouths of the hungry snakes below.

Using the skills he learned in Aetheria, Mooney minimized his weight and was striding on top of the crown canopy of the forest. He was running so fast that the ships had been remaining in his sight all the time; finally he saw that the ships were coming to a stop on the open grass fields several miles away from the edge of the forest.

Before landing, the Ündian ships hovered for a while above the grass field. Sherlyn looked out of the window and saw that there was a strange, circular piece of bare land that had an area of more than two acre and was surrounded by taller grass. One by one, the ships landed around the bare land; a tall scaly man was first to hop on to the ground. This man had red fins lining from his forehead to the end of his backbone, and he ordered other men to carry some white boxes and tubes out of the bottom of the ships. Now Rich and the three youngsters had got off, too, and they followed the scaly men to the centre of the circular bare land.

Now Mooney had got to the grass field and was hiding in the forest behind it. Peeping through the leaves, he was shocked to see that his friends were present; he then recycled his capsule, went out of the forest and sneaked onto one of the empty ships.

As Sherlyn entered the circular bare land, she saw that the air was twirling above her in an abnormal manner. She began to see an unstable image in the air and was starting to feel dizzy. 'Does the image in the air ring a bell for you?' asked Rich. 'I think you've seen many in books and on TV perhaps – it's an image of a crop circle. I was totally shocked the first time I came here.'

At the signal of the red finned scaly man, the other men surrounded the centre of the bare land and stretched their hands out. Like lightning, strong electric currents were generated from their gloves and directed to the spot at the center of the bare land – a circular metal plane rose slowly out of the ground. This plane was about a foot thick, and had a surface diameter of about fifty yards. On top of the panel there were strange engravings, and on the sides of it there were small holes from which steam leaked out. The strangest part of this plane was that it had

The Mission of Mooney Rooney

a closed circular gate at its bottom, which was surrounded by holes with raised edges. Sherlyn asked Rich what the panel was, but he told her to keep quiet and just watch.

The plane moved to a certain height in the air and stopped. The air above the land wasn't twirling anymore, while the illusionary image was becoming more stable – it was really one of the crop circles Sherlyn had seen on TV. Like the opposite poles of two magnets, the centres of the crop circle and the top surface of the metal plane were locked together. Now the scaly men carried the white tubes they had brought and inserted them into the holes around the bottom gate of the plane – at once the plane gave out blinding light, and the gate at its bottom was slid open. A shaft of air current was generated from the ground, launched through the gate and pierced straight into the centre of the image of the crop circle, which became apparent to Sherlyn that it was not an illusion anymore.

'That's a real crop circle, not an image!' cried Sherlyn. 'They've created a Leap Hole between Ündia and Valeor!'

'But why is their business related to crop circles?' said Jing.

'I think that the crop circles are some seals the Emissary has put between Ündia and Valeor,' said Sherlyn.

'But why do they have to open it now?' said Jing. 'Or...unseal it?'

'It's because they have to take you back, along with the spirit spheres!' said Rich. Jing trembled at the thought of what the spirit spheres might be.

'They use the spirit spheres to invade our minds!' shouted Colin.

'That's a good assumption, Colin,' said Sherlyn, 'as Ündians cannot go through any Leap Holes themselves.'

Now the shaft of air had turned into a pillar of light. The scaly men then opened up the white boxes they had brought – at once numerous objects like spherical moon jellyfish were released to the air. These

175

objects were no larger than human fists, and they floated in the air like jellyfish jerking in water.

'These are the spirit spheres,' said Rich in a low voice. 'The Ündians will make you stand inside that light pillar; and as you rise toward the gate, the spirit spheres will come to you like moths at a fire, attaching to you like leeches and go home along with you.' He then saw several Ündians walking towards the youngsters. 'They are coming!' He said.

'Time for a revolt!' said Colin.

But as Jing began to carry out his Ba Gua trick, two strokes of silver light dashed across the sky above them. Landing on the piece of bare land, it was two silver ships had the same shape as the ones the youngsters rode on earlier. Two men with light-green scales came out of the ships and ran to the red finned man. As they were talking, they stared fiercely at the three youngsters.

'I've seen these people before,' Rich whispered. 'They're the agents of the Highest of Ündia.'

'The Highest of Ündia?' exclaimed Jing. 'That means—'

Looking extremely angry, the scaly men tightened their gloves and walked to the three youngsters. 'Oh, darn!' Sherlyn shouted. 'I think they've discovered our identities!'

Without thinking, Jing spun out the Ba Gua trick and knocked down the several men in front of him. But the men got up from the ground immediately and shot out electric currents from their gloves – Jing took Rich by his arm, stabbed his stick onto the ground and leapt up to more than twelve feet. Holding Colin, Sherlyn sprang back to avoid the currents, which punched the ground and created a deep well on the spot where the Valeorans were standing half a second ago.

Suddenly, a rain of red marbles fell on the bodies of the Ündians, whose skin caught immediately on fire. The three youngsters turned and rushed to Mooney in joy. They continued to throw the red marbles

The Mission of Mooney Rooney

at their enemies, burning them all into madness and chaos. 'Colin!' he shouted.

Before Rich could be sure of what was going on, he had found himself sitting on a flying cloth. But the Ündians were shooting so skilfully that Reddash could seek no way out of the malice.

'There's no more marbles!' shouted Mooney.

'Linger here for as long as you can, Colin,' said Rich suddenly. 'They can't hold it anymore.'

'What do you mean?' asked Jing.

'Just watch, Jing.' said Rich. 'Just watch.'

Abruptly, the scales of the Ündians began to turn red, and electric currents had ceased to come out from their gloves. Scratching their scales like mad, the Ündians ran around crazily in circles on the ground below Reddash.

But as the lucky Valeorans cheered for their victory, a rainbow-coloured halo rose slowly out of the lake far away...

Chapter 23
The Map

Not knowing where he should be going, Colin flew Reddash over numerous forests and mountains. Rich was constantly praising his piloting skills, but he held on tight to the margin of his cloth and spoke nothing. He felt that the unexplainable bond between himself and Reddash was now so strong that not even death could separate them.

'Hey Colin, slow down – where're we going now?' asked Sherlyn.

'To find the Hengestone of course,' said Mooney.

'Yes, but where is it?' said Sherlyn.

Nobody could answer this question. 'Rich,' said Mooney, 'do you have any idea?'

'I never knew it existed until yesterday,' said Rich.

Mooney sighed. 'Would it be hidden in another city?' he said.

'Another city?' said Rich. 'I heard the scaly people say that the nearest city is really far away from ours – it's impossible for them to reach there without some special vehicles. Well, I think those Aetherians wouldn't have made such a mistake by telling you to come to a wrong city.'

'You're right,' said Sherlyn. 'We should trust Muloka. But Rich, can you think of any special places the Ündians have talked to you about?'

Rich lowered his head and was in thought. But as he was about to say something, a strong electric current was shot down on the left side of Reddash. The five of them lifted up their heads, and saw a great, rainbow-coloured halo flying soundlessly above them! Not waiting until it attacked again, Reddash accelerated forward at Colin's bidding.

'Let's hide in the forest!' said Jing.

'There're snakes down there,' said Mooney.

'Does anyone have a compass?' asked Rich suddenly.

Mooney quickly took out a compass from his backpack and handed it to Rich. 'Head southeast, Colin,' he said. 'This halo is the one we saw on top of the rod-like building in the city. It is the symbol of the Lord of the city – apparently the Lord has got to know all about you.

'I remember this place I read about in an ancient Ündian book. There's a great shining stone located somewhere in the southeast, but nobody in modern days has seen it before. I don't know where we are right now, but I reckon that we shouldn't be too far away from the lake city. We could as well just give it a try and head to southeast for the shining stone.'

'Wow, you can even understand ancient books,' said Jing. 'That's so cool, Rich.'

'When I get bored I just go to the library and read,' said Rich. 'Actually, the library itself is ancient already, since the scaly people don't use it anymore.'

But now the halo was coming very close behind Reddash and was beginning to shoot out currents again. Sherlyn looked at Mooney's backpack and remembered something. 'Where are our propellers?' she asked.

'Propellers?' said Mooney. 'They're in Jing's bag. But why? We can't use them now – they're for the Hengestone.'

'If we died now, then who's going there to find the Hengestone?' said Sherlyn. 'There're four propellers – we can use two of them!'

Agreeing with Sherlyn, Jing took out two cubic propellers which were no bigger than his own palm. He quickly positioned them at the back of Reddash and pressed the buttons on them: at once the cloth was boosted up to twice its normal speed. But danger was lying ahead...

Not far before Reddash, there stood a strange canyon like a wall so wide that it seemed to have no border. Overruling normal physics laws and properties, the grey air above the gap of the canyon was being sucked violently and continuously downwards, while the dust the roof of the canyon was not affected at all. It looked as though a great curtain of vacuuming air was being pulled straight down from the sky and into the deeps of the canyon gap.

'Jing, put away the propellers!' shouted Mooney. 'We can't go through the vacuum wall – we'll get sucked in.'

'Can we go around it?' asked Jing.

'It's too wide,' said Sherlyn.

'We can go over it, then?' said Jing.

'That's impossible,' said Rich. 'The clouds in the atmosphere here are different from those in our World. There're lots of charged particles embedded in the clouds; and if we go too high up, we'll be hit and killed by lightning.'

'But what else can we do?' said Jing. 'The halo is getting near behind us!'

'We can walk through it,' said Colin.

'Walk?' said Jing.

'Yeah,' said Colin. 'As we can see from here, the canyon gap itself is not too wide. I can make Reddash become a little bigger and cover the gap with it. Then perhaps we can walk over the gap having Reddash as a bridge.'

'That's impossible!' said Mooney. 'See how the air is being sucked into the gap? I'm not sure if Reddash and withstand so much pressure.'

The Mission of Mooney Rooney

'We have to give it a try,' said Colin. 'Come on, Reddash!'

So the five of them landed on the roof of the canyon and got off of the red cloth. Colin sat on the ground and whispered something to Reddash, which then stretched slowly towards the vacuum wall along the floor of the roof. The front region of the cloth was bending upwards in order to withstand the sucking force from below; after some struggle, Reddash had successfully reached the other side of the canyon, temporarily cutting the vacuum wall into halves. 'Look!' cried Sherlyn. 'The halo is here – let's cross the gap!'

So she crossed the red "bridge" hand in hand with Colin, followed by Jing, Rich, and at last, Mooney. But as Mooney was still running on top of Reddash, the halo had already reached above the canyon shooing out an electric current with great accuracy – as Mooney jumped instinctively over to the other side of the gap to avoid the blow, the current struck heavily on Reddash and knocked it off of the edges of the canyon gap. At once, the red cloth was consumed by the vacuum, while the accelerating halo had no time to put on its brakes and crashed right into the vacuum wall. Exploding into pieces, the colourful halo was gone forever out of the sights of the four youngsters.

Colin stood on the other side of the canyon, wordless. Then he burst into tears, crying in his uttermost voice the name of his best friend. Deep in his heart, he knew that Reddash had been alive all along, like a person, who had had a soul that reflected Colin's very own. But now he was gone, just like Colin's parents, and would never return again.

'Hey Colin, what are you doing?' said Sherlyn. Wiping his tears with his sleeves, Colin turned his body around slowly and looked at Sherlyn, who suddenly realized something and screamed, 'No––!'

Reacting as fast as possible, Sherlyn and Mooney threw everything to the back of their minds and ran towards Colin – but it was too late.

At the tipping of his toes, Colin flipped himself backwards and dove into the vacuum wall. Sherlyn and Mooney watched the complete horror of the body being sucked straight down into the deeps of the canyon until the vacuum wall seemed to be separated into two again, while Jing felt weak and dropped to his knees. The wailing cries of Sherlyn lingered long in the air.

Mooney held Sherlyn tight in his arms. At that moment, nothing remained in his mind, except the memories of the boy with the amazing cloth. He remembered the first time he landed on the cloth, and the first time he held the boy's hand – he thought that they'd be friends for life, and that the four of them would always be together no matter what, but–

But this is life, Mooney. People would be leaving you at any moment, no matter who they are, who you are.

Suddenly Sherlyn remembered something. 'The blue stone!' she said. 'The Monitor's wish stone!' Like mad, She searched through her backpack for it. 'Here it is!' she said. Holding it up in the air, she closed her eyes and made her wish. 'Please, please bring Colin back to life!' But nothing happened even after a minute. 'It's a lie!' yelled Sherlyn. 'It's a lie…' Angrily, she threw the stone into the canyon gap. Loosing her consciousness, she fell like a feather into Mooney's arms.

Not knowing how much time had gone by, Mooney felt a hand on his shoulder. He turned, and saw that it was Rich. 'It's getting dark,' said Rich. 'Let's go – you still got things to do.' But Mooney didn't move.

Rich took a deep sigh. 'Okay,' he said. 'We can stay here for the night.'

With Sherlyn still in his arms, Mooney sat down together with Jing and Rich on the roof of the canyon. All the world seemed silenced.

The Mission of Mooney Rooney

The next morning, Rich stood up and said to the youngsters, 'Cheer up! Colin wouldn't be happy to see you all like this. He'd like you to continue your mission without him, right?'

The three of them lifted up their heads and looked at Rich. They got up slowly and decided to cast away the burden of yesterday and pick up their backpacks again. But they had no idea of where they should go.

Suddenly Jing saw something twinkling on the far land beyond the forest below them. 'Look!' he said. 'What do you think that is?'

'I think that's a reflection of light on a piece of metal,' said Rich. 'I'm not sure but it's possibly what we're looking for!'

'Let's go there first, and we'll come back here to stay with Colin again,' said Sherlyn.

'Gee, but I'm tired,' said Jing.

So Mooney took out the pyramid and refilled enough energy for Jing, Sherlyn, and himself. He proved that it worked for Rich as well, as the man was full of spirit again after putting his palm on the device and inhaling deeply. 'This energy can maintain in your body for a few days,' said Mooney. 'But now let us carry you over there.'

So Mooney and Jing put Rich on their shoulders, minimizing their weight using Aetherian skills. Along with Sherlyn, they jumped down the cliff of the canyon and strode lightly on the top canopy of the forest. Since it was too early in the morning and the black snakes were still asleep, the youngsters had no problem in finding a straight path toward the twinkling object.

Now that they had come before a small hill, it became apparent to them that light was coming from behind it. They quickly climbed over the hill – they were dazed to discover a great desert, and on which a structure that shone brightly right in front of them.

'What a beautiful piece of architecture,' said Sherlyn.

'It's made out of gold, isn't it?' said Jing.

'Oh I see...that's why it's shining so bright,' said Rich.

But Mooney scratched his head. 'But why a pyramid?'

"Pyramid" was the best word to describe this object. It wasn't as big as those in Egypt, but its shape was similar to them, except that it was an octagon at its bottom and had eight sides to it instead of three or four. Seemingly, its surface was all gold, polished; despite the fact that the sun in Ündia was so dim and pale, the pyramid still shone like a light in the dark.

'Would this be the shining stone in the book I read?' said Rich.

'It doesn't matter,' said Jing. 'There's nobody else here – let's get down there and have a look at it.'

So they slipped down the hill and ran to the pyramid, which they thought was about three hundred feet tall and fifty yards wide. They examined the lower region of the structure, and found that it was made up of three levels of gold bricks, each about three feet tall. Taking a closer look at the bricks, Jing noticed that there were thick horizontal lines deeply engraved on each level, and that the lines on the same level were facing each other end to end. With a big smile on his face, Jing ran around the pyramid, yelling, 'This is an ancient Ba Gua! It must be!'

'What are you talking about?' said Sherlyn.

'Look at the bottom three levels – they're a scrambled ancient Ba Gua!' said Jing.

'What is an ancient Ba Gua?' asked Mooney.

'Oh, I should've explained that to you,' said Jing. 'The ancient Ba Gua is said to be discovered by the Chinese people when the world began. It's basically a diagram of a balanced system of eight elements of life, and it has been mysteriously used to predict the future. Well, you don't have to understand how it works. Its structure is quite simple though...let me draw it out for you on the sand.

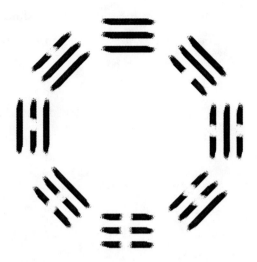

'Each of the eight "elements" is represented by a three levels of horizontal lines of different lengths. But now the lines are all scrambled on the pyramid.'

'We can get all the lines back into place and see what happens,' said Mooney.

'How are we going to do that?' said Jing.

Mooney lowered his head and was in thought. 'Remember the type of lock some people use at school?'

'You mean those that you can twist the numbers around for the right combo?' said Jing.

'Yeah,' said Mooney. 'We can try twisting the three levels around.'

Although the pyramid looked very solid, the three youngsters found it extremely easy to move the levels around with bare hands. Since the top of the three levels was too high for them to reach, they had to climb up on the engravings on the lower two levels in order to move it. However, after they had twisted the bricks to the correct positions according to Jing's diagram, nothing seemed to happen.

Jing shook his head. 'Sorry guys,' he said. 'Probably I'm wrong about this Ba Gua idea…'

Mooney went over and put his hand on his shoulder. 'It's not your fault, Jing,' he said. 'Anyway, we should continue to try heading southeast. I should take out my compass and figure out the direction again.'

'Direction!' cried Jing. 'Yes! I forgot about direction! The ancient Ba Gua works only if it's facing the right direction. Come, let us move the bricks again!'

So they repositioned the gold bricks according to the direction shown on the compass; and behold! the earth started to shake below their feet, and as they cuddled together, they lifted up their heads and saw that the gold pyramid was rising slowly out of the ground, revealing some markings on the place where it was standing.

About three feet in height, the markings seemed like a three dimensional picture that was composed of packed sand. But since the area of the picture was so large, Mooney suggested that they should climb up the hill behind them for a better view. They all agreed that it was a masterpiece of art as they looked down from the hill, but it also came clear to them that it was indeed a map, a delicately constructed one.

Chapter 24
Cave Behind Waterfall

'This map looks familiar to me,' said Sherlyn. 'Isn't it...the map of North America?'

Sherlyn was right – the raised portion of sand in the middle of the map had the exact shaping of modern North America. She also noticed a strange silver spot sitting somewhere on the sand map between modern Canada and the United States.

'That silver thing looks like mercury,' said Jing.

Suddenly Rich saw something at the foot of the map. 'Look!' he said. 'There're some ancient writings down there!'

'What do they say?' asked Sherlyn.

Rich narrowed his eyes. 'Hm...it says..."huge...water...behind"... and there's a word I don't know in the middle of the sentence.'

Abruptly, the earth shook again, and the pyramid was lowered back into place on top of the secret map. The lines of the Ba Gua spun at an amazing speed and were all scrambled up again as soon as the pyramid had reached the ground.

'That's it?' said Jing. 'So, "huge water behind" is all we've got?'

'Well, let's look at it in a more positive way,' said Sherlyn. 'This map is apparently using the spot of mercury on it to indicate the location of

187

something. And let us assume that the "something" is the Hengestone we're looking for.'

'But what exactly does that spot represent?' said Rich. 'Why does it have to be mercury, not something else like a piece of solid metal?'

Mooney thought for a bit, and then looked at Rich with his eyes wide open. 'Water!' he said. 'The mercury spot indicates that the place is a body of water...'

'Would it be a lake?' said Sherlyn. 'I remember the location of the spot – it is somewhere among the Great Lakes!'

'But it says "huge water behind,"' said Mooney, frowning. 'If "huge water" is a lake, then what can go "behind" it? A lake lies flat, and it doesn't really make sense if you say that a thing is "behind" a lake.'

'Then, could it be a body of water that somehow stands vertically?' said Sherlyn.

Mooney's eyes widened even more. 'Yes!' he said. 'A waterfall! Yes! If it's near the Great Lakes, then it must be the Niagara Falls!'

But Jing took a deep sigh and said, 'But how are we going to get to the Niagara Falls? Plus we're in Ündia, not Valeor.'

'I remember Muloka has said that the shaping of land is all the same in the three Worlds,' said Mooney; 'it's only some of the geological features that are different. So it's not hard for us to get there if we can find out where we are right now.'

'Hm...let me make an assumption on that,' said Sherlyn. 'Well, I think that the underwater city we lived in is probably the only city in North America, since Rich has said that it's almost impossible to travel to another city from it even with the rocket ships we rode on earlier. And, since the Ündians are so intelligent, they should very possibly have built the big city inside the largest of the Great Lakes – Lake Superior, corresponding to Valeor's geology.'

The Mission of Mooney Rooney

'The circular piece of bare land was located south of the underwater city,' said Mooney. 'And we fled southeast from the bare land and came here. To my knowledge, the Niagara Falls are located on the Niagara River, which flows from Lake Erie into Lake Ontario. Therefore, in order to get to the Falls, we should fly north.'

'But the vacuum wall is in our way if we head north,' said Jing.

'We can head northeast,' said Mooney.

'That sounds like a good idea,' said Sherlyn. 'Let's go now.'

But Rich hesitated. 'You guys can go,' he said. 'I don't carry special abilities like you, and I'd just be a burden if I come with you.'

'Of course not!' said Sherlyn. 'Remember that we're all on the same boat? You've come with us all the way from the city – we won't leave you behind!'

'I'm old,' said Rich. 'You already have to carry great responsibilities on your shoulders…' Sherlyn buried her head into Rich and was in tears yet again. Rich smiled.

'To be honest,' he said, 'I feel very honoured to be able to help you. I am very glad that I could still contribute to the planet, even though I am old. But I believe that you can finish your mission without me.'

Mooney sighed. 'If you really want to stay here, Rich,' he said, 'you could. And we'll come back for you as soon as we have found the Hengestone. Here – refill enough energy from this device, and I'll put you in a safety capsule in just a moment. We'll be back, perhaps in a few days – it won't be long.'

*   *   *

Minimizing their weight again, the three youngsters ran like the wind toward northeast. Not knowing how much distance they had covered, they felt that their feet had become mechanical, running blindly towards uncertainty.

It was about noon when Jing turned around and shouted, 'On our far left!'

Sherlyn agreed with him. 'That must be Lake Erie!' she yelled.

With great speed, the three of ran pass Lake Erie by its east shore and saw that Niagara River was not far ahead. 'The Falls!' cried Jing. 'I see it! The Niagara Falls!'

It was the first time Jing had visited the great falls. 'It's grandly beautiful,' he said.

'What?' laughed Sherlyn. 'You're lucky, Jing. The Falls here in Ündia are so much more beautiful than that in Valeor. See all those ancient trees along the banks of the river? In Valeor we can only see resorts and other facilities.'

'Sherlyn, we're not here for sightseeing,' said Mooney. 'We're here for the Hengestone behind the Falls.'

'Be more romantic, Mooney,' said Sherlyn. 'By the way, shouldn't it only be solid rock behind the waterfalls?'

'No – there are some other possibilities,' said Jing. 'A waterfall could destroy the weaker portion of rock behind it and create a cave inside the wall of the cliff. A cave formed like this is called a "rock shelter."'

They found a rock platform among the cliffs of the Horseshoe Falls. The sound of the galloping water was so loud that they had to scream on top of their voices as they spoke. 'Okay,' yelled Sherlyn. 'Now how can we locate the cave, since the waterfalls are so big? Are you sure that we can go through the water?'

'We'll have no problem going through the water,' said Mooney. 'But if we chose the wrong spot where there's no cave behind the water, we'll hit on the cliff and die, probably.'

'Well, we can use this,' said Jing, taking out his stick. 'If I really lost you, stick, I'd be thinking of you even in my sleep.' And he threw the stick to the right side of the Horseshoe Falls.

190

Like a needle, Jing's stick penetrated through the waterfall, hit the cliff behind and bounced back to its master, who aimed a little left and tried the same method again. After a few more trials, the stick finally went through the middle section of the waterfall and did not come back again.

'Oh gosh,' said Sherlyn. 'The stick's got flushed away by the water!'

Jing lowered his head, and his nostrils widened. 'Don't worry man,' said Mooney. 'It probably just went through the water and entered the cave we're looking for. Come on – let's jump into the cave.'

'I'll go first,' said Sherlyn. 'You know, if the stick really got flushed away...'

Mooney smiled bitterly. 'I don't want lose another friend,' he said. 'If we are to go, we'll go together.'

So, with Sherlyn on his left and Jing on his right, Mooney held hand in hand with his best friends and jumped together toward the waterfall. Like flying, the three youngsters leapt through the air and hit their heads first on the water. Grabbing tight on each other, they closed their eyes and held their breaths...

'Aw! This hurts!' said Jing.

Mooney opened his eyes and could see nothing. 'Where are we?'

'I think we're in the cave,' said Sherlyn, smiling. 'Can you still hear the waterfall? It's just too dark in here.' She then took out a bright object from her backpack and lighted up the entire cave.

'When did you learn to steal, Sherlyn?' said Mooney. 'This glowing marble...'

'I took it from the underwater city,' said Sherlyn. 'I...saw that it was pretty, so I wanted to bring it home with me.' Jing laughed.

Looking around, they found themselves inside a cave, whose opening was covered by a huge curtain of water. Seeing that his stick was jammed between two rocks, Jing ran over immediately and pulled it right out.

But after some time of searching and inspecting, the three youngsters could find nothing but unmovable rocks inside the cave. Mooney sat down on the floor, dazed. He knew it – he knew that he was wrong about every assumption he had made. Now he was utterly defeated – so helpless, clueless, and aimless.

Sherlyn sat by his side. 'Don't give up,' she said. 'Remember all the decisions we've made together? We've never been wrong.'

'I know,' said Mooney. 'But I don't understand. According to the map, there's at least something hidden in here…at least there should be some traces, but…'

'Could it be that the Ündians have already taken the Hengestone away to remove all traces?' said Jing.

'Taken away?' Mooney's voice cracked. 'Taken away…how do the Ündians take the stone…oh, I get it now!' He jumped up all of a sudden and held the hands of his friends. 'I get it now: we've interpreted the map in a wrong way. It's not an Ündian map, but a Valeoran one!'

'You mean the Hengestone is in Valeor?' said Sherlyn.

'Yes,' said Mooney. 'Because if the Ündians cannot travel to Valeor themselves, how can they manage to bring the Hengestones from Valeor to Ündia? They can only attach spirit spheres to Valeorans and control them like marionettes and tell them to hide the Stones.'

Jing scratched his head. 'So the Hengestone is at the Niagara Falls in Valeor?'

'Yes, I'm sure,' said Mooney. 'Let's go back to Valeor now!'

He took out the Leap Hole detecting device and found a Leap Hole not far away east from the cave. But Sherlyn said, 'What about Rich?'

'Oh!' said Mooney. 'I almost forgot about him. Well, let's go back and get him first, and then we'll leave Ündia together. Let's go!'

The Mission of Mooney Rooney

So the three of them took a deep breath and launched out of the cave. But as soon as they emerged out of the waterfall, their momentum ceased, and they started to fall straight down to the river below. Strangely, the air around them seemed to have become like a sticky mass of jelly as they fell, which then hardened and held the three youngsters in midair, squeezing every single inch of their flesh. As they rolled their eyeballs helplessly around, they saw that there were over five hundred Ündians standing like ants all over the cliffs and shores. Among them, a man with light-green scales, wearing a small rainbow-coloured halo on his head, carried out a constant kneading motion with his fingers, seemingly to be controlling the tightened air around the youngsters.

Suddenly Mooney heard a voice talking directly to his brain. 'I'm the Lord of the city of Zudkonan, and I clearly know why you have come here. Although I admire your effort and determination, I am sorry to tell you that you are not going to succeed. Already Valeor has demolished itself a long time ago, and we, Ündia, are going to rebuild it. I am sure that you would love to help us reinstall the loveliness that once existed in your World.

'But as you can see, nothing has worked out for us – first of all, we Ündians deserve a much better place to live than this one. Do you know, my dear youngsters, that we were all the same in the beginning when we came to Earth as Immigrants? How unfair it is for us to have become Ündians, you Valeorans, and them Aetherians – can't we just stay the same forever?

'It's not fair – indeed, it has never been fair. Who says we're all equal? We did not choose to be Ündians. If all our destinies were assigned by pure chance, why does it have to be us? Why did the Immigrants have to be separated into three races in the first place?

'We cannot hope for fairness on this planet. The only way to unite the three Worlds is to let the spirit of Ündia walk on every corner of Earth. It would be wise if you join us now – or you will be destroyed.'

But Mooney struggled to send out a thought. 'All you've been talking is just selfish – you want Ündia to be the best. Hatred has consumed you! Believe in your destiny; have faith in the scheme behind all things!'

Then he felt a great pressure exerting on his body and putting him into tremendous pain. He felt that his muscles were flattened and pressed against his bones, and that his skull was on the verge of explosion. Just as he was about to realize that all was over, he felt that the pressure around him was all ceased. Wondering if he was now in heaven, a place where he had always dreamed of, he faintly saw a blue spot of light in the sky above. Through the narrow crack of his eyelids, he recognized the image of two beings sitting on a familiar object...

* * *

At the tipping of his toes, Colin flipped himself backwards and dove into the vacuum wall. His body travelled quickly down the gap and hit finally on the bottom-most floor of the canyon.

Numerous air-sucking holes were entrenched on the floor like small volcanoes. Strangely enough, the holes underneath Colin's body seemed to have stopped working, dividing the vacuum wall narrowly into two.

Suddenly a soft voice called out Colin's name and told him to wake up. The boy then opened his eyes and saw a stone sitting on his chest, giving out blue, gentle light that surrounded his entire body. Turning his head to the side, he saw Reddash, torn like a piece of useless garment. He picked it up and held it tight in his arms – it was cold and lifeless. He then held the blue stone in his hand and recognized it. 'Wish stone,' he said in tears, 'you know that I can't bare such a loss. If you are able to, please bring him back to life and let us out of here!'

He lifted up the stone and let its light reach every corner of the canyon gap. Slowly, the red cloth started to stir as the blue radiance

The Mission of Mooney Rooney

showered its face; once again, Colin seated on his cloth and launched out of the gap against the vacuum.

But he never knew that the wish-granting stone could also help him break through physical barriers. Hoping to reunite with his friends, Colin headed southeast and reached the golden pyramid. Filled with unspeakable joy when he saw Colin, Rich could only jump up and down in tears of delight inside his capsule. Hopping onto Reddash, he showed Colin the direction where the others had gone...

* * *

With the wish stone glistening in his hand, Colin broke loose the Ündian air-trap and rescued his friends. Lying on Reddash, the three youngsters thought that they were either dead or dreaming. But they woke up; seeing that the Ündians were fierce and great in number, Sherlyn shouted, 'Fly to the east!'

Activating the gliders underneath their feet, the entire army of Ündians lifted up from the ground and flew at full speed at their target. Mooney immediately recycled Rich's capsule and let him speak. 'These gliders should be newly invented – I haven't seen them before,' he said.

Using the old trick, the Ündians shot out strong electric currents from their gloves, attempting to seize the red cloth. Jing quickly took out the two propellers they used last time; but as he was about to clip them onto the cloth, Colin tilted Reddash ninety degrees to the left in order to dodge away from an attack – the propellers dropped out of Jing's hands and fell into the river. 'We can't use the other two no matter what,' said Mooney, who started to sing in loudly in his clear, beautiful voice, calling upon every insect out of their hidings.

Reddash descended immediately as an enormous black cloud appeared in front of it. It was a swarm of over a trillion bees, locusts, dragonflies, beetles and other flying insects, clashing head on to the Ündian army. Many of the Ündians didn't expect such an attack and lost control of their gliders. They fell through the air and into the forest below, becoming the supper of the giant black snakes. Filled with wrath, the Lord of the city of Zudkonan opened his mouth wide, took a deep breath and blew out red flames from the deeps of his throat. The flames were expanding so fast that it consumed all of Mooney's insects in five seconds, serving a roasted dessert for the giant snakes below.

The Lord of the city stretched his hands above his head and directed two beams of lightning to the sky. The charge particles in the clouds answered his call by generating a massive thunderstorm. The small halo also detached from his head and chased after the cloth, shooting strong currents in all directions.

'I can't hold on anymore!' shouted Colin. 'How far is that Leap Hole?'

'It should be somewhere around here,' said Mooney.

But the small halo was getting very near. Jing had no choice but to pull out his stick from his back and throw it at the halo. On the other side of the cloth, Sherlyn pointed at an unusual formation of air in front of her and shouted, 'The Leap Hole!' Mooney then took out a rod-like device and shot a beam at the Hole. Muloka had told him that Valeorans were unable to travel from Ündia to Valeor unless the Leap Hole was in contact with ultrasonic particles.

Seeing that his stick was chopped into six pieces by the halo, Jing fainted and fell to his back on Reddash, whose front end had already dipped into the Leap Hole. Knowing that the halo was going to seize all of the youngsters before they could escape, Rich, dauntless as an ancient warrior, jumped out of Reddash and embraced the halo in his arms. Falling through the air, the old man could hear the screaming of the youngsters fading slowly away...

Chapter 25
The Hengestone

Clouds were stirring like whips of cream, while sweet breeze was sweeping gently across the fresh atmosphere – it seemed to the youngsters now that these simple things were indeed the most valuable.

Jing slid open his eyes in tears. Mooney and Sherlyn lifted up their heads and stared into the sky above, lamenting silently for Rich. Like a feather, Reddash lingered sadly in the air...

'Hey, what's that thing up there?'

'It's a kite!'

'No – it's a piece of cloth!'

'It's a UFO!'

The youngsters were awakened immediately from their reveries. 'We haven't finished our job yet,' said Mooney. 'Let's go and look for the Hengestone; we won't let anyone down, will we?' Confirming the direction, they flew straight to Niagara Falls.

Instead of Ündian soldiers, the youngsters looked down to the Falls and saw hundreds of Valeoran spectators aground, as well as sight-seeing boats across the water below the Horseshoe Falls. But none of these people had ever expected that an object, crucial to the World's future, was hidden right behind the waterfall, and that four nameless heroes of Earth were hovering soundlessly above their heads.

'What if there's no cave behind the waterfall?' said Jing. 'Let me try and–' He put his hands on his back but could find nothing.

Sherlyn put her arms around him. 'Don't worry Jing,' she said. 'After we've find the Hengestone, we'll go to China together and ask your Shaolin master to make you another one.'

'That's right, Jing,' said Mooney. 'Even if we died hitting on the cliff, we'd have no regret, since we've already done our best together, as best friends.'

So the four youngsters grabbed on to Reddash and headed straight for the cave behind the waterfall…

* * *

Holding Sherlyn's glowing marble, Colin managed to brake on Reddash just before it hit the end of the cave. The youngsters got off the cloth at once and saw a big circular pillar lying flat on the floor of the cave. They walked slowly around the pillar, stroking it gently with their fingers. Suddenly they looked at one another and burst into tears and laughter – they ran crazily around the cave giving each other hugs.

But Jing said suddenly, 'Is this really it? I mean…is it real?'

Terminating the celebration, Mooney went over to the pillar and looked at it carefully. It was about thirty feet in length and two yards wide. It had a surface that looked so smooth and flawless that it didn't seem like stone – it was black and shiny like a giant piece of carbon crystal.

With her back facing the curtain of water, Sherlyn gave a pushed to the pillar with her hands. To everyone's surprise, the pillar launched forward and thrust heavily against the back wall of the cave. At once the entire cliff was shaken, and water splashed onto the faces of the spectators outside who screamed in terror of an earthquake.

'Hurry!' cried Mooney. 'Let's just take the Hengestone and go!'

Attaching the remaining two propellers onto the sides of the pillar, Mooney, Colin, Sherlyn, and Jing mounted themselves one by one onto the Hengestone, and were all ready to go. But Jing said, 'Are you sure that two propellers are enough, Mooney?'

Mooney scratched his head. 'Well, just in case,' he said, 'we can tie Reddash around it.' And Colin did so.

Jing activated the propellers. Zoom. The four youngsters held on tight to their Hengestone and were boosted out of the cave.

On the way to the Stonehenge in England, Jing lay comfortably on the pillar and fell soundly asleep. Mooney noticed that Sherlyn was silent, so he bent over to her and said, 'There're many things we still don't understand. Wait until we go back to Aetheria, we'll have a long talk with Muloka.'

'But I just want to know something now, Mooney,' said Colin. 'Why didn't the Ündians bring the Hengestones to Ündia?'

'That's because Ündians cannot travel to the other Worlds,' said Mooney.

'And why is that?' said Colin.

Mooney smiled. 'I don't know,' he replied.

'Oh, and, why don't they have guards around the Hengestone?' said Colin.

'Guards?' said Mooney. 'I've never thought of that.'

'Actually,' asked Colin again, 'why didn't the Ündians just destroy the Hengestones?'

'......'

Colin laughed. 'Should we go home for dinner tonight then?'

'You're hilarious...'

'......'

...

Printed in the United States
83198LV00003B/58-105/A